SLUMBERING

BOOK ONE of *THE STARLIGHT CHRONICLES*

C. S. Johnson

I write for an audience of four—J.C., my mother, Ryan, and Chelsea.

But this is also for Sam, my favorite almost-superhero in high school, and Mr. Shoemaker, our ninth grade math teacher, who named you accordingly.

To Get *Awakening* (A Special Christmas Episode of The *Starlight Chronicles*) as a bonus for picking up this book,

Or download It At:

https://www.csjohnson.me/awakening

" … For to whom much is given,

much shall be required … "

Jesus of Nazareth

C. S. JOHNSON

THE STARLIGHT CHRONICLES

☼Prologue☼
Wingdinger

The winter winds were cold and harsh, laced with particles of hail and snow. The air was dry, the sun was hidden, and just from looking at it, I could tell Lake Erie was in the freezing temperatures. Apollo City, along with the rest of northern Ohio, was covered in a blanket of gray-white snow/slush, but city inhabitants were still trying to go about their humdrum lives with as little interruption as possible.

I had to say, the *eela*—shadow monster—rampaging all around the city wasn't helping. Not in the least, if you can imagine it.

As he hovered in midair, today's choice of monster giggled as he began attacking another crowd of people. He'd shown up a few times this past week, but this was the first time I'd gotten close to killing him without breaking curfew or skipping class.

Not that I minded those things, of course; I just minded getting in trouble for them.

This sinister-ling is Daikan. He "specializes" in cruel humor, but not the kind I liked or agreed with; some of his material was *really* lame. He'd been nicknamed "The Jester" by the local press—anything to get sales up without infringing on Batman's legal rights.

While he certainly reminded me of some kind of ex-con carny, there was a villainous twinkle in his eye all too reminiscent of his many demon predecessors and his fearless Sinister leaders. Not to mention there was the same cringe-

7

worthy delusion laced in his laughter.

"Ha-ha, I told you I would have you rolling with delight sooner or later," he cried out mockingly, as indeed, the crowds rolled over, though in pain. "Daikan always has a trick up his sleeve!"

Who knew who he thought he was talking to? Some people were snapping photos, while others were running away screaming. All of this chaos was happening, of course, while I was attempting to destroy him.

Unfortunately, this was nothing out of the ordinary. It was just a typical day in the life of the superhero known as "Wingdinger." Me.

My fingers gave an icy snap as I clenched my fists. "No one's laughing down here," I retorted angrily.

Just so you know, I had a right to be angry. Daikan had largely ignored me that day, and only paid attention long enough to laugh at me. And the third-person referencing was getting old.

"Watch your back, kid," Elysian, my "pet" changeling dragon, thundered at me. He swooped down and curled protectively around me just as Daikan slashed out his attack.

Spindles of power trickled through the sky, swiping over us as Elysian ducked and I dodged. There was a sudden break as a nearby tree fell and I heard something—probably one of the old city park buildings—crumbling behind us.

"Let's go," Elysian muttered, ignoring the glare I gave him

THE STARLIGHT CHRONICLES

as he leaned down to let me up on his back. But I, reluctantly, climbed on.

I wanted nothing more than to fly on my own two, irritatingly useless, wings.

As Elysian took flight, the wind bit at my face, matching the bite in my tone. "Look who's laughing now!" I taunted, tackling the laughing trickster right out of the air. Something puffy and squishy gooped through my gloves as I no doubt punched through a lung, knocking the wind (along with other substances) out of his body.

"Ugh … Gross." If only this were some kind of video game, I thought ruefully. *Me and the guys would be all over it.*

A split second later, I was thrust back into the fight. Several events blurred through my mind as the end of the battle became eminent.

Flinging the pus off of my fist …

Elysian's brief approving sneer …

Falling from the sky, tangled up with the demon body …

Ah, the welcoming rush of adrenaline. I'd become quite the junkie since this started.

I grinned to myself; I liked this trick. After several months of fighting off these monsters, I no longer had any fear of falling.

Instead of freaking out like I used to, I clawed my way on top of the evil *eela,* forcing my enemy down even more as we slammed into the ground.

Jolted but still standing, I victoriously wiped a spray of dirt off my face. "Ha. Got you!"

Elysian scuttled over. "Good work, kid. I think we did great today."

We? I rolled my eyes.

Elysian had spoken too soon. Or maybe he jinxed me, because the next moment, Daikan propelled himself upright with more power than I'd thought possible, sending me flying back through the air as he roared angrily.

"Ugh." Of all the places to land, it had to be in a pile of frozen dog poo. "Gross." *Why did I always have to land in something completely revolting?!*

I looked up just in time to see Elysian unleash an attack of his own. My dragon's bright celestial fire hit its mark as I stood up and hurriedly tried to clean myself up. Being a superhero is not as important as looking like one, in my opinion.

"Augh!" Daikan cried, the dragon fire slowly eating away at his colorful clothes and sizzling into his wrinkly skin. Even though I love my barbeque, it was a gruesome sight to watch him flap and burn. It probably would have been more enjoyable if he was dead. And plucked.

"Finish him!" Elysian called out.

"No one defeats me," I murmured, letting myself smile. *For once, we are going to get along all right without—*

10

A hot, blazing arrow of light suddenly soared out of nowhere. It struck the demonic creature in the head, unleashing a small bright explosion and bombing out brain residue. I jumped back and shielded my face. When I peeked over seconds later, Daikan was gone.

I groaned. I'd thought too soon. *She's here.*

Following the trajectory of the arrow, I looked up. And there she was.

Starry Knight, skillfully perched in the trees, was looking down on me, both literally and figuratively. "I told you to stay away from this business," she called out in a disdainful greeting, as was her per usual.

"Oh, just go away," I stomped my way over to my supposed counterpart. "I was doing just fine until you showed up. *And* I was here earlier than you."

"You are just getting in the way." She glared back, tightening her lips, obviously irritated. "It's clear you still don't know much about them, do you, *Wingdinger?*"

Since I was pretty sure she was making fun of me in addition to insulting me, I bit my bottom lip angrily, raging for blood. That was just like her, to disregard all the effort I'd espoused trying to learn more about the different demons suddenly plaguing our city. Believe me, between the *eelas*, the *tenwaleisks,* and the *bakreels*, I'd had more than enough outer dimensional demon instruction.

But even so, who really cared if I didn't know that much yet? All I really knew for sure was that I had to fight them.

That had to count for a lot of it—over half of it, really. And the other stuff, well, I'd figure it out later, when I had the time and/or the inkling to care.

Starry Knight jumped down from the heights of the tree. "Since you appeared, I've had to save you more than I've had to defeat these monsters."

"Hey! I got some of them, too," I protested. *At least two or three, anyway ... out of ten or twenty or ... Who's really counting here anyway?* "I would've had this one, too, if you hadn't stolen my chance!"

"I'm sure you wouldn't have been able to do it," Starry Knight replied, waving me off. "You haven't gotten any stronger in the last weeks. Just give up and leave this to me. Oh, and I'd make sure to get some stain remover on your clothes." She flipped her long hair over her shoulder before she flew off, her stark white wings beating gracefully.

The embarrassment and anger burned, steaming hot. I thrust my fingers into my "wingdings" at the sides of my head, for which I was named, and tried not to scream. The pain of tearing at my feather-crown didn't help.

And neither did Elysian, of course. (He never does, trust me.)

"Don't worry about it, kid," Elysian told me. "You'll get the next one."

"What if I don't?" I asked sharply. "What then?"

"Don't do this to yourself. She's not worth it." Elysian

12

transformed. As a changeling dragon, he had the ability to transform into any reptile, but he often just pushed back his wings, sucked in his big dragon belly, and shrunk down to the size of a small lizard or chameleon. It was handy for travel purposes, I had to admit, but more often than not it meant he was nearby. And I didn't really like that.

"Maybe she's got a point. *She* seems to be getting more powerful." I doubted Elysian had noticed the increasing intensity of Starry Knight's arrows in the past few weeks. I also doubted he'd be able to refrain from making some irritating comment about it if I brought it up.

"Don't forget, we don't know much about her," Elysian said, honestly and exasperatedly. "If you really think she's getting more powerful, it could be a problem."

"You think?" I snorted distastefully. *Of course she is a problem! She'd been a problem since day one.* "How do you think she does it? How do you think I can get strong enough to beat her?"

"You're supposed to be concerned with the demons, so forget about her."

"You know what I mean."

"Frankly, I agree with Starry Knight; it's your own fault you're not getting more powerful."

"What?!" My gaze blazed into Elysian's, and he (wisely) shuffled back a few feet. "How can you say that? You're the one who's supposed to be 'mentoring me' or however you put it."

"I cannot teach a know-it-all!" Elysian glared at me. "Look, you've accepted the task of defending the world from the Sinisters, but you're still as arrogant and self-centered as you always were. And it's worse since you've been given the powers. You still rely mostly on your guesswork to get the job done."

I motioned to my uniform, my transformed self. "Selfish? How can you say that? Do you know what I'd rather be doing while I'm fighting off the forces supposedly bent on destroying the world? I could be on a date!"

"Ugh! You make this so hard!" Elysian sighed. "You might have accepted the truth of your destiny, but there's more to believing than just accepting the truth. There's more to power than strength."

I muttered out a string of curses, probably a bit too loudly for Elysian's taste, because he chastised me a moment later. "You could get a lot more powerful if you just had some self-control."

"What do you mean by that?"

"I mean you can't even control your language, or your anger, or your actions. No wonder the demons laugh at you! You'll bring about your own destruction soon enough with that kind of attitude."

Before I could respond, the large clock tower in the city chimed, and I had another reason to hate my life. "Aw, great! It's after my curfew! Cheryl and Mark are going to be upset. Can tonight get any worse?"

Almost as soon as the words were out of my mouth, Elysian piped up with a half-smug, "Here comes the press."

And right on cue, a desperate-looking journalist hopped out of some nearby bushes, followed by several more of his camera-wielding posse. "Excuse me, Mr. Wingdinger, sir, can we get a couple of questions?"

I immediately ran for cover.

"Stop! We need to talk to you!"

"Come back, we want to make a deal! You'll be rich!"

"Where's Starry Knight?"

Anyone could tell you I was not usually shy in front of the camera. But the last thing I wanted was to do was to take financial responsibility for all the buildings and vehicles and other stuff that had been damaged in the previous months, and the blame for all of the people I hadn't saved. These were the major reasons I ran away from the press and cringed at the thought of interviews.

"Come on, Elysian," I said quietly. "Fly us away from these soul-suckers."

Elysian cocked an eyebrow at the irony and smothered a laugh, transforming once more. Moments later, we were safe and out of reach.

THE STARLIGHT CHRONICLES

How did this all happen? How did I manage to get drafted into humanity's last defense in an interdimensional war?

Truth be told, I wasn't exactly sure how it all began. All I really know was the day this mess exploded into my life, I'd been thinking about much more important matters. Much, much more important matters …

☼1☼
Normalcy

Three Months Before

I was thinking about the intricacies of life, and how simple it was to control them, if handled with efficiency and precision, how there could be no surprises, no mistakes.

But I knew there wouldn't be any mistakes; after all, there was no true right and wrong. Everything was relative, and relativity only called for adaptation. I knew this as sure as I knew the sky was blue, and Taco Tuesday at my school cafeteria was invented by cannibals. It was as real as the game device in my hands, or the air in my lungs.

Anticipation mounted, and my heart started to skip. The last piece of the puzzle was seconds from touchdown when—

"Dinger! Put that game away!"

I nearly flew out of my seat at the sudden interruption of my Tetris game. I luckily (skillfully) remained cool, merely snapping my eyes up to meet the discerning stare of my tenth grade AP American History teacher, Mrs. Smithe.

I had to grin, because her darkened eyes were burning over the top of her thick, black-framed glasses, and I knew she was annoyed. This was not the first time, today or otherwise, she had stopped, mid-lecture, to remind me to pay attention. In her world, no matter how addictive the game was, it was supposed to come second to her teaching. "Supposed to" being the operative phrase.

17

"Aw, but I'm so close to beating this level." I smirked good-naturedly.

The silent, deadly expression I received told me it was clearly not one of her good days, so I shrugged carelessly, smiled brilliantly, and tucked away my Game Pac. I even decided to graciously wait ten more minutes before pulling it out again. Mrs. Smithe seemed reassured by this illusion of obedience, and went back to teaching. She was always a bit of a control freak, but I've never really met a good teacher who wasn't.

And for all her trouble, Mrs. Smithe—Martha—was probably my favorite teacher at Apollo Central High School. She was middle-aged, with short curly hair that almost stood on end when her teacher-senses were tingling. I supposed it was her glasses that really gave her an authoritative demeanor, since her short height and tiny bone structure did not. And she always had coffee nearby. I once figured out while I was bored in her class that she could support a small company stock all by herself. You have to admit that's impressive. If I had any problems with her, it was that she just didn't seem to understand that Tetris was the ultimate meaning in my life.

I'd played the game for years, and it was the key to unlocking the secrets of all life—that we were all just players, some of us winners, a lot more of us losers. That there was nothing more to life than filling it with fun, and working to fit all of the pieces together cohesively, in order to claim glory and the right to brag. It was a beautiful, meaningless thing, the epitome of my preferred existence.

Plus having the title of Tetris King was a nice touch—I'd

thought "Tetris Emperor" was a bit much.

"Psst, Dinger."

I turned toward my friend, Evan von Ponce—whom I nicknamed "Poncey" awhile back and everyone, of course, universally accepted—to see he was wearing a pair of glasses he'd no doubt pilfered from a nearby nerd. "What is it, Poncey?" I grinned. I knew what was coming.

"Put that game away—now!" Poncey mimicked Martha almost exactly, with his own bit of dramatic flair added for effect.

I attempted to keep my chuckles in, but to no avail. A matter of seconds later, the inevitable reprimand came.

"Dinger! Ponce! Do I need to separate you?" Martha scowled at us, reminding me of a time when my mother actually used to act like a mother to me. All the other students in the class glanced over at us, and I played it cool, but the tension was thick. A few of my classmates wore smiles of smug superiority, while others tried not to be the next ones to giggle.

It was really nothing different from the norm. Every day it was something else. Class stopped because of *someone* talking or playing games, and the intellectual lecture was traded in for a behavioral one.

But there was never a day when Martha punished me or any of my friends with a detention. Which, in all fairness, she was supposed to do. She'd always been fond of me and my cronies.

Despite that, however, Martha tightened her lips in irritation; she had to put on *some* show of authority. "May I continue?"

"Sure, Mrs. Smithe," I assured her, though my laughter was still trying to poke its way out of my mouth. "What was that about the American colonies?"

"That was ten minutes ago. We're discussing the new country disputes now. Pay attention, Hamilton Dinger!"

Ugh. I hated it—and still hate it—when people use my full name. Or even my first. Trust my parents to come up with the weirdest name in all of history and give it to me. I was a victim of bad parenting and awkward social trends. My name said it all.

Martha turned with a militaristic air toward the front of the room, continuing with her presentation. "Okay, then ... In his farewell address, President Washington clearly advocated for the unification of political parties and a policy of isolationism ... "

Her words faded as I fell back into boredom in record time. I thought about pulling out my Game Pac again as I'd essentially blown off the lecture. I was not worried; I would read the chapter later, and then I would ace the test. That's how it was. That's how it *always* was.

Not that I'd complain. Being the class genius was fun. And being popular was, too. It was nice to be a regular on the "Apollo Central High School Hot List" organized by the cheerleaders of the so-called "Social Elite." Which was basically just the cheerleaders.

20

It was nice that I had more than my share of charisma, and probably more than my share of good looks, too. I *was* voted "Best Eyes" in the last two yearbooks.

It was great that I was, at sixteen, famous for my high school career as a football player on the Apollo Central Falcons. (I'm sure you can look up my world record.) But what I was most well-known for was my trademark smirk, the one with the power to transform me from teacher's pet to troublemaker, to instantly irritate a saint or charm a viper.

There were some who didn't appreciate my commentary, my skills, or my presence. That happens a lot when you're popular. Someone is always ugly, or jealous, or both, and they take out their insecurity on you. But I figured *someone* had to be popular, and I had to say I was very good at it. So it was my duty, my curse and blessing, to be so. And frankly, that's the way I liked it.

"Yo, Dinger."

I turned to see Jason Harbor, a member of my inner circle of friends. Jason was on the football team like me, and one of my most competitive rivals for MVP each year. But considering I've been playing sports practically forever, that really wasn't as much of a compliment as it seemed. "Yeah?"

"You coming to the Falcons' party tonight?"

I nodded. "Sure am. Still gotta tell Mark and Cheryl though. Supposedly, she'll be home early tonight, but I'm not going to hold my breath or anything."

I honestly can't remember how long I'd been on a first-name basis with my parents. It wasn't that I didn't love them or anything, because I supposed I did (sort of). It's just that their years of parenting, the parts which didn't come with a bill or some kind of other payment attached to them, were well over with.

"Sweet." Jason cautiously glanced back at Martha before telling me, "Poncey's coming over early to help set up. You wanna come? Simon can pick you up."

"Nah, it's okay. It's not too far to your new house."

I'd lived across the street from Jason nearly all my life, ever since I moved to Apollo City with my parents. But Jason's dad had recently lost his job, so Jason and his family moved away from our ritzy, upscale neighborhood to the northern slums of the city, where it is considered "more cost-effective to live." (That means it's for poor people, but I wasn't going to make discriminating judgments like that on a friend; I was content to save those for other people at school.)

Because of the awkward subject, I focused on a more substantial concern. "I still can't believe Cheryl and Mark aren't letting me get my license until I'm eighteen."

"Well, you *were* caught trying to break into your own house at two in the morning," Jason reminded me with a smile.

If you knew the story, you'd think my parents should have been turned over to social services for excessive punishment. But after it was told so many times and exaggerated in so many ways (to legendary status), I was quite bored by it. "I forgot my key at Poncey's. It was a simple mistake."

"Breaking down the back door and setting off the indoor sprinkler system was a simple mistake? I'm still trying to figure out how you managed that."

"Ah, shut up," I said, glaring. I must've had this rage-fueled look on my face, because when Poncey interrupted the conversation, Jason's expression involuntarily looked relieved. (It's well known people who argued with me usually ended up being hated in some form or another; whether I encouraged it or not was another matter, of course.)

"Did I hear you're coming to the party, Dinger?" Poncey asked, his expression pathetically eager.

It was always endearing to me to know my friends depended on me as immediately as they did food and water, so I humored them. "Sure am."

"I hear Gwen's going to be there."

At the sound of her name, I felt my heart give a happy jolt. I'd never thought, at that point in my life, that there was only one true love for me. It seemed like people who thought there was only one person for them out there were narrow-minded, and kind of shallow. Or really picky.

I really just wanted someone who would love me and fit well into my life. And I didn't think this would be too hard for me to get. (I never had a problem getting them—it was always getting *rid* of them that was the problem.)

I was Hamilton Dinger, after all. I was smart, strong, and hot. Who wouldn't love me? Who wouldn't change her whole life around to fit into my world?

23

But I was sublimely happy, nonetheless, at the thought of Gwen. There was no girl in the world who could compare with Gwen Kessler, in my own humble opinion. I'd searched and compared enough girls to know she was the perfect girlfriend for me. She was cute, and smart, and athletic, and she agreed with me on mostly all the right things. She had been the one who had nicknamed me "Hammy," saying it went well with my "cocky, devil-may-care attitude."

And on top of all things, I was more than happy to ask her out. I contentedly leaned back in my chair. "Cool."

Mrs. Smithe effectively ruined the chance for my friends to rag on me about Gwen; I was able to tell by their expressions they were looking forward to it, too. I didn't blame them. Let's face it, it wasn't often they got to do it.

"Okay, class. Before we go, our first history exam is coming soon," she announced.

Everyone groaned. Immediately, whispers and concerns were voiced without appreciation. I refrained, but only because I knew I'd pass it without a hitch.

Mrs. Smithe ignored the complaints. "It's on everything covered in the book, lectures, and notes I've given you. It's worth fifteen percent of your grade this marking period." Then she looked down her nose at all of us, eyes narrowed. "And this exam is not curved, so bribing Dinger to stay home will *not* help you."

Half of the kids in the class rolled their eyes, while the other half snickered. Hoshi Tokugawa, the exchange student from Japan, groaned. "Darn, I was saving my money for that, too."

All of this happened while I basked in a sea of my own satisfaction. It was well known that I had the highest grade in the class.

"Hey, Jase," Drew McGill spoke up. "What time are you going to be ready for the party?"

"Around seven. Don't forget to bring your video games, okay?" Jason sat back, relaxed. "After all the arguing over which ones to bring, you can't forget them. I don't want to have to kill you."

"Yeah," Poncey agreed. "Nothing says, 'Let's go Apollo Falcons' like a stack of pizza, buckets of ice cream, and hours of playing *Death Raiders III: Alien Slayer.*"

"Parties, girls, and school-wide fame. Ah, I'm glad to be a football player," Drew sighed happily.

"Not to mention all the trophies we get," I added, trying not to sound too smug.

"You mean *you* get," Jason shot back. "You're the best player on the team. The rest of us suck, man."

I knew that, but I liked to hear it as often as possible. "Well, there's no denying I can smoke you guys on the field. But I'm not as good as all of you at other things. Even though I can't really think of anything at the moment." Attempting to be humble was hard, due to my insincere tone and the large smirk on my face. "Still, football's fun."

"Very true," Evan agreed. "And it's cool to watch the

cheerleaders. Some of them are pretty fast, if you know what I mean."

Before we could laugh, a classmate of ours, Guy Fitch, butted into our conversation. He was tall and lanky with glasses, and hung out with uncool people a lot. I couldn't help but pity him sometimes. Fitch tried so hard to be popular, it's really a shame how bad he was at it. I sighed inwardly, preparing for the usual misplaced Fitch comment.

It came as expected. Fitch smiled. "Yeah, I'll say. One time, I saw this girl start running down the track, trying to tackle this kid who'd stolen her hot dog."

The guys and I gave him a weird look before laughing awkwardly. It was clear Fitch didn't understand Evan's statement. Really, it's no surprise, I thought pityingly. Fitch didn't seem to get anything. I sometimes wondered if he just acted stupid, or if he really was that dimwitted.

Oh well. Either way, it didn't really matter. He'd never be popular like me, so I didn't have to worry about him.

The bell rang, and everyone headed out of the room.

"Dinger!" Mrs. Smithe called. "Come over here a moment."

I walked over to her desk, pausing for a moment to wave to my friends. I watched as Evan waved back. His elbow hit Brittany Taylor in the process, causing her books to go flying all over the floor as she fell. Evan was too busy laughing to help her pick up her things.

I had to literally choke down a chuckle at the scene. Mrs.

26

Smithe wasn't a good person to go to happy, when you were pretty sure a reprimand was coming. And I was pretty sure it was coming. "Yes, Mrs. Smithe?" I put on a charming, eager face, wide-eyed with innocence. "Do you need me to run an errand for you?"

"Dinger, I understand you aren't impressed with my class." Her tone had some bite to it, so I knew I needed to tread carefully.

"That's not true," I argued. *Not completely true.*

"Put your lips in park, Dinger," she snapped lightly. "I know you're capable of learning. You have the shortest attention span, yet the highest grades. You must've been born under a lucky star."

I grinned. "Thanks."

"You know that's not a compliment," she replied. "Luck and miracles can't get you through life unless you die young. I can't have you being a distraction in my class. You want more work?"

"No."

"Fine." She paused here momentarily. I saw the hardness on her face leave as genuine concern replaced it. "Your mind is a gift," she told me. "But if you don't start to use it, you're going to lose it."

"I thought I was," I replied in my best non-confrontational voice. It was good that I was an exceptional student, because otherwise I don't think she would've bought it.

"Not in the way of common sense," Mrs. Smithe huffed. She scrunched up her nose and added, almost as an afterthought, "Or manners, come to that."

I smiled shyly, giving her the goody-goody face. "I understand, Mrs. Smithe. I'll be a better example."

"Good. I'll hold you to that."

"Cool. Well, I got to go. See you later!" I waved good-bye, closed the door, and a victorious sneer crawled across my face. *Another one bites the dust!*

Semantics are wonderful. It wasn't for nothing was my mother one of the most influential lawyers of Apollo City— probably the whole state of Ohio, too.

I'd set a better example, all right—next year, when time just seemed to be more convenient than it was at the moment. After all, my life was absolutely perfect—except for a few minor things, like my parents, and my brother, and all the unpopular people who thought I was just awful so they could sleep better at night. Why bother risking a change?

At the time, I didn't really believe that anything outside my control would change my life. Or at least, not in a significant, substantial way. My life was all about myself, and I figured I had complete control over that. Anything that happened outside of my control was more or less because I let it happen, and didn't feel like stopping it.

It's funny how one disaster of epic proportion can really make you change your mind.

☼2☼
Irritation

My groans echoed loudly throughout Jason's small play room as Poncey, Drew, and I all wrestled with Jason's old couch. "Man, Jase, what did you do to this couch? It smells like a fart factory exploded on it."

The guys beside me half-chuckled but that did nothing to improve our situation. It was close to party time, and we had to get everything set up, despite the obstacles we faced— namely, the large, oversized, over-smelly couch.

"It's perfect for gaming." Jason grinned as he made his way into the room, hopping over the big blue couch stuck halfway in the door. "You guys can put it over by the window."

Drew, Poncey, and I all looked at him as if he had five heads.

Jason smirked. "Oh, all right, I'll lend you weaklings some muscle."

A few shoves, a lot of heaving, and some inappropriate comments later, the couch was in perfect position for maximum television interaction. "This is really going to be big with the gamers coming," Drew said, pumping his fist into the air triumphantly. "And I'm going to beat all of you!"

"Doubtful." I laughed. "You know I'm the reigning champ."

"Yeah, yeah. Enjoy it while it lasts." Drew smiled widely, almost eerily. "I've been practicing."

"Speaking of practicing, I told Mikey to come early," Jason spoke up.

"Why did you tell him to come at all? It's not like we need him," I scoffed.

A moment of silence passed in its usual awkward fashion. Everyone knew Mikey was not my favorite person at the moment.

"Well, he's stuck in detention today, so I thought it would be good for him." Jason's soft-spoken response was weak. Really weak.

Poncey jumped up from his seat on the couch, suddenly inspired. "Dinger, you gotta hear what he did to Elm's student teacher today!"

"You mean the short, skinny, underfed German girl, Poncey?" My face broke out into a large smile as I conjured up a picture of the latest eyesore in my biology class, Ms. Nolte the Dolt. "Oh really now? Tell me about it."

"Mikey decided that it was wrong to dissect animals this week—"

"Probably because he failed the dissection quiz on Monday," Drew interjected from the floor as he untangled the game controllers.

Poncey laughed. "So Mike decided it was only appropriate for him to help other students learn the parts of the frog's anatomy—"

"Because he was just *so* concerned for the other students

31

and all—"

"And what he ended up doing was, he took all the frog's innards and laced them together, and then he strung them all around the room," Evan said. "It was so hilariously funny, too, because at first, Ms. Nolte didn't even know what it was."

"He'd hung them like Christmas tree lights," Drew explained. "With some randomly thrown here or there. Ms. Nolte was having puppies by the time that class was over. She kept finding organs in odd places. Can you imagine her finding stray pieces of dead frog months from now? Awesome. Mikey's a genius."

"I heard a cockroach was even chewing on a frog lung," Evan added.

"Cockroaches don't eat meat, Poncey." I shook my head. "That's absurd. How did Ms. Nolte find out it was Mikey?"

"That know-it-all Brittany said it was you, me, and Mikey."

I cocked an eyebrow, hinting at my non-surprise. "Oh really? So Mikey took the fall for us, huh?"

"Well, it's not like you did it, right?" Drew asked. "We know goody two-shoes Poncey here wouldn't be caught dead in detention. You wouldn't do anything like that either, would you?"

"Maybe, maybe not." The rest of them just rolled their eyes, and for some reason, it made me more than a little ticked. But I graciously laughed it off. For once.

32

"Well, anyway," Poncey spoke up, "Mikey's serving detention today with the drama students. They were there till five today, doing set work."

"Poor Mike. Detention with the drama students … " I feigned sympathy for him, though I suspected some of it was real. Between the awkward director, the poor selection of plays, and the limited special effects, drama was the worst to deal with. Our school drama department, Apollo Central High Entertainment, was abbreviated as ACHE for good reason.

The front door barked open, and I turned to see another one of my friends, Simon Gangel.

"Hey. You're late, man," Drew scolded.

"He was probably in detention for checking out the math teacher again." I laughed.

Simon put on his lopsided grin. "Guilty as charged, Dinger. But I'm way behind in Ms. Darlington's class, and my parents will kill me if I fail again. Plus I'll never get into med school."

"They'll also probably kill you if you get arrested for sexual harassment," Poncey pointed out.

I nodded uninterestedly in agreement, as we all got back to setting up the room. Simon wasn't the brightest crayon in the box; he's actually probably the blackish-gray one. He might've been a senior, but he was finishing up his high school career with a lot of sophomore-level classes. Simon getting into med school would only happen as a miracle—and I didn't believe in miracles.

33

Half an hour later, the Harbor's house was packed. The music was booming and loud, and it was a wonder the neighbors hadn't called in to complain. (As far as I'd heard, anyway.) The sound of teenagers laughing and yelling to each other, and even the particularly gruesome and exaggerated violence of *Death Raiders III*, was lost to the ocean of hardcore rock n' roll, our freedom song of choice.

There were close to forty teenagers at the house, though it sounded more like four hundred. There had to be a couple party crashers—that happened a lot when *I* was at parties—but Mr. and Mrs. Harbor didn't have the time to worry about it; they were too busy washing the dirty dishes stacking up in the sink, like all good parents would be. Last I'd checked, Mrs. Harbor had a sour, determined look on her face (she wasn't happy, but she was going to attempt to be as pleasant as possible until everyone went home—*then* she would unleash the monster within) while Mr. Harbor was more upset he had to help with the dishes. He kept it to himself, probably aware that if he bothered his wife, he'd get the majority of her wrath.

The party hadn't been going on long when I found myself in the middle of beating Jason at a video game involving a savage, bloodthirsty battle for all mankind and the pursuit of personal glory. (So it was kind of like high school.) A rush of adrenaline bolted through me as Jason's character finally fell

34

over, wriggling and shaking the last of the animated blood out from his severed head.

I let out an excessively loud and obnoxious celebratory, "Ha! Beat you!" before I succumbed to the overwhelming desire to laugh hysterically. I loved having witnesses to my personal successes.

"Way to go, Dinger!" Simon cheered. "I'm next!"

"Sorry guys, I already called it," Poncey declared, tearing the game controller out of the hands of a disgruntled Jason.

"Poncey!" I smirked to see such a willing victim.

Shouts of "Poncey!" "Ponn-cey!" and "Pon-eceya!" echoed through the room. I smiled. My friends would often imitate me. It was highly amusing, if not sad for the lack of originality.

"You got it coming, Dinger. I've figured out the perfect fighting strategy," Evan bragged.

"Oh, really now? Well, I doubt it'll work, but what the heck? When you're declared the loser, I promise I won't rub it in your face for more than a week or two." *Or three or four. It really depends on my mood.*

The match started, and the guys gave encouraging support with an orchestra of armpit noises. Jason, still upset at losing to me, led the cheering for Evan with a "Poncey" whoop.

My smirk grew wider as I landed a costly blow on Evan's fighter. "Ha, got you!" I boasted. "Looks like your theory of how to beat me isn't working quite yet, unless it's to not do

35

any hard work and hope I beat myself."

Poncey just grinned. "I haven't applied it yet," he replied, before his head suddenly turned toward the door. "Oh! Hi, Gwen!"

My head whipped around, only to see an empty doorway. It took me less than a moment to realize I'd been duped, and it was even quicker that anger and frustration set in. "Oh, man!"

In the seconds of effective distraction, Evan had managed to land numerous blows on my guy. I cursed loudly a moment later when Evan won the match.

"Oh! Oh! Oh!" Drew guffawed. "You got served, Dinger! Sweet move there, Poncey. Genius!"

Poncey wallowed in the glow of his triumphant victory as my face was no doubt hot-coals red. "Yeah, I won!" he bellowed uninhibitedly, like some screeching balloon that popped.

I inhaled deeply, and then shrugged my shoulders, like it was nothing—which it was. "You got lucky," I remarked scathingly. "Cheater."

"Hey, don't be a sour-butt, Dinger," Poncey teased me. "Just because you're jealous of me and clearly vulnerable to the opposite gender, that's no reason to be all cranky. In fact, it's perfectly natural."

"Oh, shut up, Poncey. You and your delusions are enough to make me sick."

Drew grabbed the controller out of my hands and bumped me away. "I'll give you a *real* challenge, Poncey."

Ha. I doubted it. I'd just beat him before taking down Jason. "You guys suck," I announced. "I'm going to find more appreciative company."

On my way out, to make things even worse, I bumped into Via Delorosa, the head cheerleader at Central.

Via instantly frowned and snapped, "Watch where you're going, Dinger!"

"Sorry," I muttered as I ducked quickly out of her way. Apologizing was the best thing to do in this case, and since I actually was truly regretting running into her, it was not even a fake apology.

I was ashamed to admit it, but I had dated Via during the previous year. We were a power couple in the ninth grade, before I broke it off. Via had hated me ever since. (Even though she would still occasionally hint at me to get back together with her.) She was still especially mad because others really played it up as being her fault. In reality, I was more than willing to agree—there was no way I'd ever consider loving someone so shallow and superficial. I'd dated her for four months before telling her I "didn't know what I wanted." (Meaning, of course, I knew she wasn't what I wanted.)

I was even kind enough to do it during summer vacation, so she would only have to face the prospect of initially being embarrassed at cheer camp instead of school. You'd think after all my kindness to her, she'd go easier on me. But no,

37

she didn't.

I involuntarily shuddered at the memory of kissing her; it'd been like tasting raspberry-flavored dirt.

I made my rounds throughout the party, talking and laughing with my fellow football players, mostly about how our chief rivals, the Rosemont Raiders, were so lame. I grabbed some grub, flirted and winked at the pretty girls, told some stories, and compared Tetris notes with some of the guys. Everything was going well.

I should've known up to that point something was going to go terribly, terribly wrong. Later I would think that if I could pinpoint a moment in time where all was well with the world, and then all of a sudden went awry, it would be around the time I first met *him*.

I wasn't five steps away from re-entering the game room when I heard Jason call out, "All right, Tim! Beat him!"

"Who's Tim?" I muttered as I walked into the room. There was no Tim on the football team. It crossed my mind that it was probably some loser from school who was hoping to name-drop me later in a conversation where he'd be trying to impress a girl. Again, that was one of the few problems with being popular.

"Hey, Hammy!"

I lost all trace of eminent disgust and suspicion as Gwen's honey-colored eyes jumped up to meet mine. "Hey, Gwen," I called, trying to contain the wave of happiness spouting up inside me.

38

Gwen was sure pretty today, I noticed. She always wore make-up and styled her hair, but she seemed to be extra-pretty today; she must've known I'd been angling to ask her to be my girlfriend.

Before I forgot, I nodded courteously to the girl standing next to her. "Hey, Laura."

"Hi," Laura replied tentatively.

Laura Nelson was Gwen's best friend, and before tenth grade, had been one of mine as well. But she was still one of Via's lackies, unlike Gwen, and she knew the rules. The cheerleaders had a ban on talking to me. (Not that they all followed through on it, but social code *was* sacred.) This was another reason there weren't a lot of girls in my inner circle of late.

"How's cheerleading going?" I asked Laura. It was fun to watch her squirm.

"Oh, it's … going okay." Laura awkwardly glanced away. "Hey, I'll see you guys later, all right?"

I watched with satisfaction as she left. *Mission accomplished.* At last I was alone, more or less, with Gwen.

Gwen snickered as Laura edged her way out of the room, excessively careful to not even bump into me. "I guess Via is still angry."

"I'm not surprised," I said. "Frankly, I'm surprised I'm still popular. It's a rare person who dumps the head cheerleader and walks away unscathed, even four months later."

"You have a point there. Please don't hold it against Laura, though. She's trying so hard to make Vice Captain before the Spring State Tournament."

"I'll consider it, just because she's your friend."

Gwen giggled again, so easily charmed. "So, how're you tonight?"

"Oh, you know." I shrugged. "Had a fight with the parentals. They didn't want me coming here tonight, no surprise. Cheryl and Mark are so ridiculous sometimes, I just can't believe it ... " I went on to explain how I'd arrived at my house after school to find, surprisingly, both parents home. Cheryl was running around trying to get ready for a business dinner, one of the *very* few ones where she was allowed, and actually wanted, to bring her family with her. Mark, fresh from a sixteen-hour shift at the hospital, was brewing coffee. And Adam, my three-year-old brother, was mostly ignored, playing "doctor" to couch pillows, various stuffed animals, and curtains.

Between my mother trying to guilt trip me between threats, my father calling for me to be "rational" between cups of coffee, and Adam humping my leg, crying, "Hammonton," and blah, blah, blah-blah, blah, it was a wonder I'd gotten out alive. I vastly enjoyed telling this to Gwen; she would appreciate me making it through my mess of a family just to see her.

Can you see why I didn't like my family? They were all so concerned with their own lives that they just didn't seem to care enough about mine.

As I recounted this story to Gwen, I watched, mesmerized, as her expression glazed over. I was thinking how cute she was, trying so hard to vividly imagine what I was saying, that I hardly noticed when she interrupted me halfway through.

"That's fascinating." Gwen smiled, the focus coming back into her eyes. "I don't know where you get your energy for all that, Hammy." She yawned.

"Coffee."

"Is that it? Gross. I'm a tea drinker."

I cringed, slightly. "Switch."

Gwen laughed, an enchanting sound I found as energizing as my beloved sugar and cream coffee. I decided my first job as Gwen's boyfriend would be to convert her into a coffee drinker like me.

"Ah, man. This sucks!"

I, along with everyone else, suddenly snapped attention back to the game, where some guy—Tim—successfully vanquished Drew's character in a horrific display of graphic violence.

"Wow, that's gotta be a record!" Evan squealed. "Drew, you sure are having some bad luck. First Dinger and now Tim? You're losing big time."

"Oh, shut up, Poncey." Drew glared at him, more than a hint of indignant humiliation in his voice. "Shut your big fat mouth."

41

THE STARLIGHT CHRONICLES

Before I could step in and assure everyone Drew felt rightfully sorry enough to let Tim win, Tim stood up.

"I'm sure I just got lucky," he assured Drew with a coddling smile. He gave Drew a friendly punch on the shoulder. "Or maybe you just felt sorry for me and let me win?"

Drew caught on, pathetically grateful, and I was instantly super annoyed. "Well, I was going easy on you," Drew gallantly admitted. "I'm getting some more soda, anybody want some?"

Not bad, I thought. I didn't know much about Tim, but I knew two things for sure: One, he was almost obsessively, single-mindedly willing to kiss up to my friends, and two, he was certainly not a football player.

It was written all over him, frankly. Tim was tall, with spikes in his hair, and a wide, crooked smile on his baby face. He wore a flannel shirt under a leather jacket. The ugliest, dirtiest cowboy boots imaginable stuck out like clown shoes. The "tough-boy" look was lost on Tim's heart-shaped face; it was more bunny than human. Puberty had certainly not been kind to him, either, I thought privately, a smug satisfaction rising.

I was just thinking about graciously asking what on earth Tim thought he was doing here when Gwen interrupted me.

"Tim, over here!" Oh, crap. Gwen had invited him.

I thought briefly how vomiting in my mouth would be the most appropriate response to this, but I held it in. *If only*

THE STARLIGHT CHRONICLES

Martha could see my manners now.

"Hey, Juliet," Tim said, smiling kindly at Gwen. He turned to me. (How appalling—he wasn't even addressed by me first!) "Hey, Dinger," he said. "English was tough today, huh? I saw you beat out your old Tetris record halfway through class."

"Oh, you have Mrs. Night, too?" I asked, surprised. I should pay more attention to insignificant details like that, I mused.

"Yeah. Her English class is … well, it's okay. Don't you think so?"

I shrugged, uninterested. "Her name's 'Night' for a reason, since everyone sleeps. I usually play Tetris the whole time."

Tim laughed. What a suck-up. "I heard you had the highest rank for Tetris scores."

I nodded, uninterested. I certainly knew how good I was.

"Gwen told me you almost got in trouble with Mrs. Smithe today."

"Martha's cool. She knows I'll ace that history test coming up, no matter how much I play." I shrugged again, bored. "So, how do you know Gwen?"

"Gwen and I are both in the school play," he told me.

"Play?" Huh? What?

Gwen hit me playfully on the shoulder. "I've told you the

43

school's performing *Romeo and Juliet* a million times already. I'm Juliet."

Ah, that play. Whatever. (Please, it's not like it's football.)

I winked at her. "So you're Juliet, huh? They need a Romeo still?"

"No. Tim's Romeo."

Ouch, that burned. "I know that." I sighed. "I just like to annoy you sometimes, Gwennie," I admitted. And then I caught her eyes with mine, allowing her to almost see past my outside antics to my deep, sensitive thoughts. She looked down a second later, a faint blush on her cheeks. Ah, yes ... Girls love that kind of mush.

"I think the play's going to be a hit this year," Tim spoke up, interrupting my calculated moment with Gwen. "We've got some students coming from Rosemont to help put the set together; it's going to look amazing when it's finished ... "

I soon decided that if I acted like Tim was of no importance, maybe Tim would realize he *was* of no importance and go away. (You laugh, but it's worked before.) I turned my full attention to more appealing matters.

"Speaking of Rosemont, Gwen, you going to the football game tomorrow night?" And I focused back on Gwen and only her. (It *is* hard work to ignore a freak show.) "That's who we're playing."

Gwen giggled. "Is that all you ever think of, Hammy?"

"Yes," Evan quipped, coming in from nowhere. He had a

tendency to do that. "Football, girls, and Tetris. That's all Dinger ever thinks about."

There were several chuckles and a couple of unsure looks.

"Do you think you'll come to the play, Dinger?" Tim asked.

"We'll definitely win," I cantered on confidently. "The Raiders are due for losing, since they are a loser school."

"Hey, you didn't answer Tim's question," Gwen said.

"Huh?" I widened my eyes in mock surprise as I reluctantly allowed myself to look at Tim. Gwen apparently wasn't picking up the cue; I was beginning to doubt her acting skills. (This did not bode well for an already-doomed play.) "Oh. Hey, Tim," I said. "Didn't see you there. You really should loosen up. Standing like that, I thought you were a lamp or something."

A wave of laughter came up from the guys around the room.

"I'm serious!" I insisted, noticing Gwen was not smiling. "Look at him, he's not even moving."

Tim rubbed his neck nervously. "Well, I did get the part of Romeo for something," he agreed after a long moment.

"Oh, right," I continued. "You're Romeo. You must be one of the best actors in school, huh?"

Gwen broke into grin, like she was happy I was being nice to this freak. "He sure is," she exclaimed happily.

45

I was suddenly trying to process how sick Gwen's face was making me when I heard myself remark, "Hey, Tim. Why don't you try acting like a football player, then? You know, since this is a party for *football* players?"

"Hammy—" Gwen started to say something before I cut her off.

"It's not like this is Broadway central," I explained.

"Hamilton—"

"I'm just saying this party was specifically for the athletes of Apollo Central High, and prancing around in tights on a stage playing a suicidal-lovesick fool doesn't exactly sound like a qualifier," I went on, relentlessly. Gwen obviously needed to be reminded of social order.

But rather than be grateful for this, Gwen frowned. She suddenly grabbed me and pulled me after her. "Excuse us for a moment." She smiled up at Tim, who had this hurt, confused look on his bunny face that was clearly overdone for extra sympathy. What a fake.

As Gwen nearly ran over Drew when he was returning with all the sodas, Drew caught the look on my face. "What did I miss?"

☼3☼
Awe

At that point, I realized the party was not going as well as I'd hoped. But if Gwen getting a little bit angry at me had been the worst thing that happened, I know now I would have been okay with that. Compared to what actually happened, I would have been thrilled, even.

Here's what *should have* happened:

Gwen should've realized I'd done her a favor, swooned into my arms, and begged me to never let her go. We would've then proceeded to dance the night away or sneak out early for our first unofficial hang-out date at Frosty's Ice Cream Parlor down the street. Then she would've agreed to be my girlfriend, we would've had a nice time, and no one would've ended up at the hospital in pain.

And then there's what actually happened:

"Hamilton Dinger, what's wrong with you?" Gwen angrily whispered—hissed—at me. "You can't talk to Tim like that."

"Why not? It's not like he's a girl or anything." I defended myself. Although he acts like one, I added maliciously to myself. "It's a guy thing, Gwen."

"No it's not! I don't see you talking to Drew or Jason or anyone else in there like that," Gwen argued, a pout starting to form on her pretty face.

Ugh. First of all, I hated it when girls would pout; it was too much of a reminder of Via's manipulative tactics. And

47

second, Gwen *clearly* did not understand the complex nature of the male mind.

"Come on, Gwen. Relax," I tried to reassure her. "Look, if I just let him into the group, then it'll only be because of you. Do you really want that? He'll have no respect from any of the guys."

"What? How can you justify your awful behavior?"

I had to roll my eyes. My mother was a lawyer; I'd known for years how to get around nearly everything with circumstantial, circular logic.

"I want this to stop, right now," Gwen pleaded, apparently tired of waiting for my response. "I don't care if this isn't how you do things. You know I like him!"

"Well—" The full impact of her words hit me like an eighteen wheeler, and for the briefest moment, the earth was flung from beneath me.

Then it passed like gas, and I looked at her curiously. "You like him?" That was going to make my proposal for her to be my girlfriend difficult for her to accept.

And there went my evening. All of it was effectively, irreversibly, and utterly ruined. I can't think of enough adjectives or adverbs to describe how completely it was trashed.

"Yes … yes, Tim … " Gwen nearly choked as she admitted it. Her cheeks flushed red. "Listen, Hammy—"

"Wow." I shook my head, sadly. She was obviously lying.

THE STARLIGHT CHRONICLES

Or she'd watched too many chick flicks lately where the girl ends up with her Romeo. "Look, I'll start being nicer, but whew, you really should really watch what you say."

"I'm not kidding," Gwen insisted, still red but not interested in recanting her stance. "I've liked him for a while now."

"Oh, really? When did he ask you out then?" I crossed my arms and leaned against the hallway wall.

I was not surprised, since my instincts had told me earlier I was not going to like Tim. He was a merciless social climber, willing to throw poor Gwen under the bus so he could skip up a few rungs. Willing to seduce Gwen and break her heart, just so he could hang out with me and the guys.

Admirable strategy, but it crossed the line. (Now, if it had been someone like Laura, I wouldn't have minded as much. But this is *Gwen*, not some preppy-go-lucky *regular* girl.)

"He hasn't asked me out yet," Gwen said. "But I don't want you scaring him off."

A dark look came into my eyes. "I told you, I'll start being nicer to the guy. I've better things to do than worry about him anyway, like the big game tomorrow, the Homecoming game next Friday, the history exam coming up, hot girls …"

Gwen huffed indignantly.

And then I knew how to handle the conversation. "I'm sorry if you're jealous, Gwen, but I have a life outside of you." My tone was highly sarcastic, sweet enough to spit

49

sugar.

I guess I should've explained Tim's social takeover plan to her, rather than call her out on her jealousy, because she entered into full fighting mode before I could stop her.

"Hamilton, I'm sorry you think that," Gwen snapped, her face getting even more red. "You know, I'm not jealous of you and your little fan club; I might have been once, but not—"

"So you admit that you do like me," I remarked calmly enough. I knew it all along.

"I don't like you that way, *anymore!*" Gwen practically shouted. "We're supposed to be friends."

"Sure, we're friends. That's why I'm protecting you. Tim's just using you to get to me," I shot back.

"Is it really impossible that a guy would like me?"

"No, but it's just all of a sudden. Now that he's met me and the guys, it's 'Oh, I think I'll hang out with Gwen and *her* friends?' Come on, you're smart enough to see through that!"

"Hammy, I've liked him for a long while now. Tim's sweet and kind and would never use me to further some hidden agenda—" She stopped in mid-sentence as we suddenly saw Tim standing in the doorway. "Tim!"

"Uh, excuse me," Tim said, his awkward tone clearly indicating he'd heard at least half of the conversation. "My mom just called. She wants me to go home now."

"But—"

"No, no. Don't worry about it." Tim gave her a nice smile. "She said it was urgent." He took her hand and gave it an affectionate squeeze, probably just to annoy me since I'd called him out on his trickery. "You stay here and have fun, all right?" He nodded to me. "Thanks for letting me come," he said, before he headed out.

Gwen stood in shock as she watched him go. I jerked her from her emotional flood as I laughed. "What a loser," I remarked. "Has to lie about his mom calling him to get away. And left you here, too! That was hardly what I'd call potential boyfriend behavior."

Gwen stared at me incredulously before she frowned. "You're just jealous!" she yelled, before storming away, heading toward the exit to, no doubt, hurry after Tim. She looked back briefly enough to add, "Tell Jason we said thanks for the party, please. Good-bye!"

And I was appalled. After all, I was the one who was supposed to be her boyfriend. I shook my head sadly. Women. "Well, she'll come crawling back to me sooner or later," I assured myself as my cell phone rang. *Ah, that's probably Gwen now.* I smirked.

"Ham? Can you hear me?" It was my father.

Disappointment flooded me like water through a broken dam. And this was another sign I should've seen indicating more trouble was coming.

"What do you want?" I sighed loudly, clearly

51

communicating my irritation.

"Ham, your mother and I want you at home," Mark replied in a calm voice.

In the background, I heard Cheryl grumbling and complaining to herself. I wondered once more how in the world I'd gotten such lame parents. "How do you know I'm not at home right now?"

"Please, son, give me some credit," Mark answered. "I know you better than you think. Are you at Josh's house or Dave's?"

"Do you mean, am I at Jason's house or at Drew's?" I huffed. "You know me better than I think, but still can't get my friend's names right? Come on. You're going to have to give more realistic evidence to support your claims."

"Ham? Hamilton Alexander Dinger, are you listening to me?"

I rolled my eyes at my mother's voice. It figured she wouldn't just sit by while Mark called. The expected rebuke came easily enough.

"You are in big trouble when we all get home, if you don't listen to me now," Cheryl bit out. She unleashed her verbal discipline over the phone, but it was muffled; an interruption of static fragmented the one-sided conversation, and I was grateful, for once, that cell phone reception was still bad sometimes.

"Cheryl, just tell the boy to get on home, we don't have the time for this now. You can battle this out as long as you want later." Mark had no doubt reached over and tugged the phone out of Cheryl's hands, a dangerous act in itself. Now he was putting himself in deeper jeopardy by attempting to tell her what to do.

"Hamilton! Your father—" Cheryl nearly spewed out the words; she's miffed by the interruption. "Your father insists we settle this later. Honey, you must leave Jason's house *right now!*"

"What? Why should I?" I retorted easily enough.

"Because there's a meteorite heading straight for Apollo City!"

A moment passed in silence. Not a word was spoken on either side of the conversation.

Then I laughed hysterically.

Mark and Cheryl must've had too much to drink at dinner. "Well, thanks for the info. See you later. Oh, watch out for flying pigs on your way home." Without a second thought, I hung up.

I was about to share my parents' delusions with my friends when I noticed the party music had ceased.

It was the first true sign of the many horrors to come that night.

☼

I walked into the living room, now full of my other friends and fellow partiers. We'd all crammed in there, staring at the television or pushing others out of the way to see the television. I saw the emergency report flashing through someone's armpit hole, and it was then that another sense of dread tingled down my back.

The news anchors began giving their report, and we were all transfixed enough that we weren't talking or whispering or even texting.

" ... Sources are confirming a red-level, city-wide natural disaster," the news anchor reported. "The expected time of impact is within the next several minutes ... "

"What? What impact?" a girl yelled. I was glad someone else was willing to look like an idiot and ask, so I didn't have to.

"I bet it's a bomb," one of the guys whispered, but not quietly enough. "It's about time for the next world war, right?"

"Listen up, everyone," Mr. Harbor spoke up. "We need to hear this."

The television newscast continued, although some fuzziness started to break up the reception. "Mapping of the intended destination of the meteorite is ... once it has made it past Earth's atmosphere ... scientists believe it has an unusual course ... "

I was certain the anchor had switched languages at that point. I didn't understand. Others around me were asking questions as well.

"A meteorite?"

"Like an asteroid?"

"A meteorite is smaller, I think."

"Do you think it will cause a lot of damage?"

"Oh, no! With my luck, my house will be destroyed."

"Hey, maybe the school will be crushed! Wouldn't that be great?"

There were several comments on the nearing disaster—no one was apparently *too* concerned, thank goodness. As Mr. Harbor went to answer the ringing telephone, Mrs. Harbor (no doubt secretly glad for a reason to terminate the party) happily announced, "Kids, if you can make it back home in less than ten minutes, get going now. The rest of you can stay here."

There were a number of moans, but there was enough of a somber overcast that most teenagers immediately started picking up their things and heading out the door.

While this was happening, I wasn't really sure how to process the news; after all, how on earth could my parents be right? It didn't make any sense.

Suddenly the world seemed a lot scarier than ever before.

Also a lot more tragically hilarious. After all, Apollo City was largely founded by a "controversial" astronomer. (Crazy, but super rich, somehow.)

A hundred or so years ago, Dr. Ogden Skarmastad bought off the northern part of the city and founded several astronomy-based research projects. He was obsessed with the idea that he could find the secrets of the universe by studying the stars. He was one of the reasons we had Lakeview Observatory. And why the northern section of the city eventually became the city slums.

How ironic was that? A town founded to discover the "secrets of the universe," only to be dilapidated by one of its small, deadly projectiles.

I could imagine the meteorite relentlessly pelting down on the people of the city, unleashing fate's revenge. It looked a lot funnier in my mind than I'm sure it would be in real life.

That's when all of a sudden, realization struck. "Gwen." Chasing after her fleeing nerd of a turd, there's no way she knew what was happening. She was in danger of being one of those people getting hit by shooting star pebbles.

Before I could talk some sense into myself, I headed for the door. I *had* to go catch up with Gwen. Nothing had ever felt so certain and so right. I barely noticed I'd almost tackled Jason on the way out.

"Dinger, wait!" I could sort of hear Jason call after me as I lunged out his door. "You'll never make it home—just stay here!"

But I hopped off the porch, and scampered down the sidewalk, finally breaking into a full run once I hit the road. I glanced back briefly, wanting to tell Jason I was rescuing Gwen, when his mother interrupted me.

"Come on inside, Jason," his mother called. "I'm sure he'll be all right."

I saw Jason as he shook his head. "All right, Mom," he said with relieved reluctance. "I'm coming."

Weeks after the meteorite hit Apollo City, I climbed to the top of the Apollo Time Tower, a strikingly-white clock tower built after the death of Dr. Skarmastad to "honor" him. (It was a condition of his will that his estranged son had to fulfill to get a hold of the Skarmastad fortune; it was also part of the will to have the tower washed and repainted every three years, or so the rumors went.)

From the top of the crystal-white tower, I could see the extensive damage from the meteorite. Ashes and pebbles of dirt were caked in the wrinkled skin of the city, and the crater left in the city was still obviously waiting for government funding. There were several rows of broken windows; I could see them even far into the distance, blinking at me like broken eyes. New construction had started on the crackled metal bones of the tallest buildings.

Only the Time Tower was spotless, a striking white nose planted on the bruised, sunken face of Apollo City.

I'd come up to think and to brood about my fate. It was the only place I could go where I felt like I would be able to concentrate on my situation properly.

After running away from change since the day the meteorite came, it was hard *to want* to take my new life seriously, or to even believe that it was for real.

Here's the thing about beliefs—*real* beliefs. They change you.

My life had always been about me, and anything that I felt was missing in my life was able to be found at the local grocery store, or in breaking a new sports record, or by dating another girl. Believing anything else about my life would leave me helpless, and I would need to sacrifice something.

I didn't think, even when the meteorite struck the earth, that I would ever change, or ever believe in the truth that began to stalk me.

It wasn't for nothing that I held the honor of being the fastest runner on the Falcons. Within mere minutes of running, I'd spotted her. Gwen was just up ahead, standing at the end of a street, waiting for the pedestrian lights to change on the other side.

58

Relief and gratitude poured through me—relief because Gwen was alive, and gratitude because Tim was nowhere in sight.

I glanced around, recognizing my surroundings immediately; this was where Rosemont's district border met with Apollo Central's district. There were usually a lot more people and cars here, but the streets were more or less deserted now. Even the building windows seemed dark and foreboding.

I had to tell myself to stop this train of thought. It was no time to be panicking or overreacting. Really, it wasn't the movies.

I called out to Gwen, and she turned.

I smiled and waved.

My smile was lost as Gwen turned back around and started walking away, this time with an air of defiance and indignation.

I grumbled silently. Why did she have to act like a brat *now*, of all times? I was the one who should be angry! I mean, here I was, coming to rescue her, and she was being such a kid about our argument, which was clearly her own fault.

The sky was already glowing brighter though, so I knew I would have to deal with her attitude later. I sighed and sped up. "Gwen!"

Gwen finally (*finally!*) stopped, though I figured it was more due to her tiny-heeled shoes than my rescue.

"Look, Gwen—"

She cut me off quickly enough. "Dinger, I'm ashamed of you," she started. (She never called me "Dinger" unless she was really upset with me.) "And appalled you would even try to come after me, even to beg for mercy, after what you said in there."

"What?" I hadn't come to apologize. Normally, I would've laughed at the very notion of it, if not for the more pressing concern of the up-and-coming death-by-meteorite. "I'm not—"

"I know you're not good at apologizing," Gwen interrupted me again. "But there's a little saying, 'practice makes perfect—'"

"No, wait—"

"No, you wait!" Gwen gritted her teeth in anger. "I'm not finished."

"Stop!" I had to wave my arms to get her to actually stop. "We'll discuss this later. We have to go. We're in danger."

By then, the fiery sky was an ominous, bleeding red. Sirens in the city started going off. Fire trucks were off in the distance, their alarms emitting a high-pitched bell. This wasn't good.

But Gwen apparently didn't hear. (Or didn't care.) "In danger of what? You really—"

"Gwen, run!" All at once, there was lightning in the clouds, fire beginning to fall on the horizon. I grabbed her arm as we ran, trying my best to keep her from tripping. Though I was forgiving of her slowness, I mentally berated her fancy-pansy shoes. Why did girls wear those things? And why did they have to wear them at the most inconvenient times?

Gwen struggled against my grip, but for her own good I held on. My grip tightened as a thundering boom blasted across the region.

It was very shortly followed by a crash. And a scream. A huge building in the distance caught fire. Then there was another loud boom, and another building burst into flames; this time, closer. "Ham?" Gwen asked weakly. "What's going on?"

I was about to tell her NASA had taken a group coffee break when I saw the meteorite itself.

Just above the horizon, there it was.

It was awing, humbling … beautiful yet terrifying, entrancing me even as I wished to run away.

The meteorite doesn't look big, I thought as I stood there, watching as it came closer. Time seemed to still as the sight held our eyes captive; with its colorful tail fluttering behind the death-black core, it assured a worthwhile way to die, and impending death has a way of being mesmerizing.

I glanced over at Gwen as she choked on a scream. Then she gaped at the looming boulder of fire above her. It was at that moment I snapped out of my trance and started running again.

THE STARLIGHT CHRONICLES

A city subway station was just around the corner; it would protect us, and it was close enough that we could just make it.

"Augh!" I cringed as I felt Gwen fall and heard her cry. Blood speckled onto the cement in small streaks. Gwen's shoe had caught on a crack in the sidewalk.

I scrambled to pull her up from the ground, but she started wailing in pain. (Right into my ear, naturally.) "Come on!" I said. "We have to hurry!"

I glanced back at the meteorite. It was close; I felt the burn of its hot, metallic fire. I glimpsed over and saw an arched doorway, and then I ignored Gwen's tearful cries as I picked her up. I couldn't tell whether my mind was reeling with thought, or if I'd stopped thinking altogether.

All I knew was that seconds later, it hit.

There was a sonic *boom* as the broken space rock crashed into the ground. Every window within a two-mile radius shattered as the array of heat and flame exploded into the ground, upheaving a hundred years' worth of life and city living.

I thought I could hear others crying out as the shockwaves tumbled through. Maybe it was me … or Gwen … it was probably Gwen.

The lights of the city flickered and went dark as the electrical current was interrupted, but I could still see. The tallest buildings in the distance were blazing with licks of fire even as the structural integrity was compromised. The meteorite had splintered as it neared the surface.

Blocks away, as the earth trembled and buildings crumbled, I huddled up in the corner of the steel doorway, with Gwen close to my chest. I was protecting her from the falling glass and the accompanying heat wave when I felt my consciousness fade, not into darkness, but into a warm, beckoning light.

I was confident, as solace overtook me, that it had been the worst night of my life.

There have been many times in my life since then, where I had wished it had all been over after the meteorite ransacked my hometown.

☼4☼
Lunacy

I felt the tingle of coldness; a drop of warmth was in me, but that was all. *Where am I?* I wondered, as I curled my legs up to my chest, hugging the warmth to me as well as I could. I opened my eyes to find I was surrounded by darkness.

Little beams of light and the twinkling of stars began to catch my attention.

I was floating, sort of … looking down. I didn't see anything below, and looking up, there was nothing above me. Stars and lights and colors flickered all around, blossoming out, backdropped against a shroud of night.

What's going on? I wondered again. Obviously, I couldn't *really* be in outer space. My breathing was regular; there was no air being crushed out by the lack of gravity.

I felt lightness all over.

Am I dead? Suddenly I was strangled by fear.

"He's been stable for hours … "

I heard voices. They sounded far away, but I was pretty sure they were close. I thought about saying something when I heard them.

A string of notes, beautifully and meticulously arranged … music soaring out to me from the far reaches of the surrounding heavens.

It was only a small, small whisper against the emptiness of

THE STARLIGHT CHRONICLES

the outer space I was in, but I heard it, and I knew it. And I knew it was for me.

I recognized the familiarity of the strange notes, and the foreign atmosphere suddenly seemed less unknown and more comforting than home.

Where was the music coming from?

"Huh?" A bright star, huge and shimmering, suddenly sparked my attention; it was unlike any other star I'd ever seen. But strangely enough, I felt like I'd seen it before, which was possible. After all, there are many stars capable from being seen from earth. Why would this one be any different?

Yet this logic failed. How would I know it was different if it was the same as all the rest?

"Did he lose any blood?" A new voice was talking now. But it was not the one I found myself waiting for.

My fingers twitched; the endless horizon of the universe curled up in my hand. Weird, I thought, studying the new wrinkles in the backdrop. It felt like cheap cotton.

"He didn't lose too much blood, Doc, but he has a small fever ... should recover nicely."

I didn't know who was talking that time, but I wanted him to shut up so I could hear the music. It was fading. But I didn't want it to go.

Then I heard it.

"I will save you, no matter the cost."

The voice—a soft whisper, one tugging at my very core. And then I could almost see … and I could almost call out a name …

But an explosion ripped through the bright star, my star, expelling all the wonders of colors and light locked away inside. I disintegrated into blinding light and accompanying pain.

"Stop!" I shot up out of bed, wide awake and covered in sweat. My breathing was irregular. I glanced around and saw the IV in my hand, and heart monitors on my chest. I was wearing an ugly hospital nightgown and smelled like iodine.

"Hamilton." Mark's voice crested over me like a bucket of ice cold water.

"Dad?" I asked, looking around.

And there he was. Mark was standing by the door, decked out in his hospital scrubs. *He must've come to see me on a break*, I realized.

It was sometimes hard for me to believe we were related. With his black hair and brown eyes, Mark didn't actually look much like me. We didn't have much in common outside of intellect and a shared coffee addiction. Still, there were times I admired him. He was a cardiologist at Apollo City Hospital—not only one of the best doctors, but one of the best paid. And it was nice that other people liked him a lot.

Mark walked over and put his arm around my shoulders. "It's been hours since you've been awake."

THE STARLIGHT CHRONICLES

"Why am I shaking?" I asked, as I realized I was shaking.

"Just a side effect. Don't worry. We've been monitoring your heart regularly, and you're doing just fine. So is your friend. She checked out of here last night. It's possible you're having a post-traumatic reaction from your recent act of bravery."

"Bravery?"

"Yes. Don't you remember what happened?"

I thought only about the dream first; I didn't feel very brave there. Actually, I'd felt something vaguely like failure and searing pain …

The sweet melody I'd heard resounding in my heart before was already disappearing, as memories of what happened earlier swarmed through my mind. The meteorite, and Gwen … someone lifting me into an ambulance, someone checking my pulse …the sandpaper feel of my body, sunburned beyond summertime …

I slumped over, putting my head in my lotion-smelling hands. So it had been a dream. "You said Gwen's okay?" I asked slowly.

Mark smiled. "Yes. I spoke with her earlier. She explained how you saved her life, risking your own in the process."

I grinned, my smirk coming back quick enough. (It was a reflex, after all.) "Oh, well. Just doing what's got to be done," I remarked. "Gwen is one of my close friends."

"I'm glad to see you're feeling better. You had a few cuts,

67

and received a nice tan, but no burns, no permanent damage."

"I feel fine now," I said. "Just hot." I didn't mention that I could feel my heart pounding in my throat.

"Well, I'm sure if you rest a while, you'll be fine. Your mother will be relieved to know you're up. She was really concerned last night." And then, as though it was timed to help dodge my biting reply, his beeper buzzed and he left.

I'll bet she was, I thought sarcastically, as I decided to drift back into sleep. Cheryl was probably traumatized at the thought of what my death might do to her business partnership.

After a few hours of napping, I heard a soft knock at the hospital room door. I had to smile when I saw who it was.

"Can I come in, Hammy?" Gwen asked politely.

I immediately had to decide between playing the charming invalid or unshakeable war hero; it was difficult because I'd seen the movies where both had worked out.

To be safe, I went with the hero one. I didn't want to downplay my role in saving her life and all that. And I could use the invalid bit later if I needed to.

"Sure." I smirked. I could tell she was in a much more agreeable mood today than she was at the party. "All my company has been my family and a bunch of nurses—mostly men, too. I could use someone I'm genuinely happy to see."

"That's not like you," Gwen said. "You like the attention. Admit it."

"No, actually, I can't wait until they let me leave," I told her sincerely. "I hate hospitals. They're so cold and deathlike."

Gwen chuckled warmly as she walked over. "I heard from the gossip grapevine that you didn't have any serious injuries," she said.

"No, just a nice tan, I was told, and some broken-glass scrapes. The nurse thinks I have a fever."

"Yeah, I had my knees taken care of," Gwen replied, pointing at her white bandage tape. "And a couple of cuts, too. But I'm okay. I'm glad you're feeling better."

"Me, too." I smiled.

"Well … " Gwen bit her lip. She was so cute, I thought appreciatively. "I came by today to … well, I wanted to thank you."

"Thank me for what?" Then my eyes widened along with my smile. "Oh, you mean for saving your life? It was nothing. I'd do it all over again."

"Yes. Thanks for saving me … " She sat on the bed beside me, patting my hand. "You're such a good friend … sometimes."

I grinned. I was just about to assure her I could be an even better boyfriend when there was another knock at the door.

I looked up to see my so-called best friend, Mikey Salyards.

"Hey there, Dinger," Mikey greeted me cheerfully. "Heard you got mangled up, and I wanted to see it for myself."

At this point, I would've loved nothing more than to throttle Mikey for ruining my big moment with Gwen, but I let it go. There's going to be enough time later to ask her out, I decided. After all, I'd just saved her life. What reason would she possibly have for saying no next time? Gwen could move on from Mr. Bunny-face Tim. We *all* could.

Mikey walked up closer and shook his head. "You don't look as damaged as I'd heard."

"I'll try harder next time." I grinned. "Maybe I'll make a quick stop at Rosemont; I *am* the Falcons' ace player, huh, Mike? That would get me really mangled."

Mikey scratched his head. "Well, I guess it would be dangerous there, but not for that reason."

"What? Is the game canceled? They didn't bench me for the season, did they?" I started to freak out a bit there, I'll admit. It'd be social suicide if I was benched or if football was canceled. It figured. My big chance to get on more-than-favorable status with Gwen, and it cost me my star role as wide receiver.

"Well, they did cancel the game," Mikey admitted, halting my spiraling. "Last night the meteorite hit right smack in the middle of Rosemont Academy. The school was devastated in the blast—it looks half-melted, if you see the pictures."

"Oh. That stinks for the game," I said, more relieved that it was *their* school that was destroyed, not my reputation and the opportunity to increase said reputation. "And well, Rosemont was a death trap, anyway. No one will miss it."

"That's horrible, Ham!" Gwen remarked, quietly disgusted. "Rosemont was still a lovely school, even if it was a prep school. We had students from there come to help with our play."

"Huh?"

Mikey came up to my other side. "Gwen's talking about the volunteers we had from the art and wood-shop students. They were much better than our school at everything."

Gwen gave him a smirk. "Yeah, you're just saying that because you like that Courtney girl," she teased. And I suddenly felt irritated, like I was left out of this conversation.

Mikey grinned. "Don't you know me so well, Gwen Kessler?"

"I take it you learned nothing from stringing frog guts around Ms. Nolte's room, then?" I asked, switching the topic to something that had my direct input available.

"Who?" Mikey laughed. "If Courtney keeps coming to the play stuff, I'm going to have to think of new antics to get into detention." He looked out the window. "You'd like her, I think, Dinger. She's tall, skinny and blonde. And pretty."

"Geez, you don't sound shallow at all," Gwen huffed.

"It's alright, Mike, you can have her," I dismissively remarked. The tall, pretty, skinny blonde sounded a lot like Via, except for the hair. "Tell me when you've changed your mind … you know, the day after she agrees to be your girlfriend."

Gwen snickered. "He's got a point, Mikey," she agreed. "You give up as soon as you've got them."

"If cars were girls, you'd have a new model every week," I added.

"One day, you're going to find a girl you like, and she won't even look at you," Gwen warned him playfully.

"Well, if Courtney keeps volunteering, that won't happen this time." Mikey grinned back.

"You know you could just volunteer to help out, right?" I asked.

"I can't have anyone thinking I'm some drama-maniac. I have a rep to protect, you know."

I was just about to ask what was going to happen to the Raiders, when Mikey turned the conversation to the window and pointed in the direction of where the meteorite had (mostly) fallen.

Wanting to see if I could get a good look, I headed over to the window. My hands grew warm as they touched the cool window glass. "What's going on over there?" I asked, beckoning towards the crater.

"I can't see anything happening." Gwen shrugged. "But I did hear they were collecting the remains for the astronomy program at the college. You know they wouldn't miss an opportunity like this."

"Do you think … " My voice trailed off as a strange feeling took hold of me—and not in the stomach, either. Something was nagging at my mind; something was wrong over there, terribly wrong.

Wait, I scolded myself. *Stop this!*

And then I really started freaking out. *Is something wrong* with me? *Am I delusional?*

Maybe that blast altered my brain more than my body. After all, there was no way on earth something would go wrong just because—

"Look!" I cried.

A sudden quake, and my train of thought ran over small, imaginary children and into oblivion.

"Augh!" Gwen screamed as black light shot out from the crater and a small explosion tussled the city streets.

As Gwen hid her face and Mikey looked away, the newly formed, turbulent, ominous clouds dispersed and flew up. And then I froze.

The clouds. They were *glaring* at me. With seemingly real eyes.

I gaped, dumbfounded. The feeling transported me back

73

into that dream, where the star had burst, and a similar cloud had taken form ...

"Dinger?" Mikey asked me, waving his hand in front of my stricken face. "What's wrong? You look sick."

"Did you see that?" I asked, horrified. "The ... cloud and all?"

"You mean the explosion?" Mikey looked too confused for me to have any hope he had idea what I really meant ...which was, *"Did you see the monster face in the sky?"*

Gwen startled me by taking my hand. "You're so pale all of a sudden. Are you in pain?"

So the answer to my subtle, disguised question was "No." Neither of them had seen it. And the question of my sanity, or my health, or just my general shock was suddenly being taken into account.

"I'm fine." I blinked as I cleared up my head and my thoughts. I tried to shake the weirdness away. *I'm going insane,* I thought. There was no other possible explanation.

In the days following my slippery slope into seeming madness, there were several incidents throughout the city which were of great concern to the police.

74

There was a man, for instance, who had apparently been mauled coming home late from work. Police were certain he'd been attacked because of the large burn marks around his wrist and shoulder. But they were confounded as to the reason why. His wallet was still in his pocket, and his briefcase had fallen underneath him; no sign of robbery. No personal vendetta could be found, save the one the man had out for his boss. No drugs were in his system, and he'd been physically healthy.

Less than a day had passed before another incident occurred in a dental office. All the workers were found looking lifeless, with rashes on their arms and necks.

Some said it was a new epidemic. Others said it was bioterrorism. There was a couple who believed it was a space virus, brought down to Earth on the meteorite. No one really believed them, but I found out later they were the ones with the closest guess.

A meteorite, a new epidemic outbreak, and a possible sociopath, all in the same week? The media was having a field day. That was probably the worst part of it all. They sensationalize *everything*.

All the "illness" victims had fallen comatose, stiffening as the days passed by. They were not dead, but they weren't alive, either. There was no way to transmit the disease, and there was no way to cure it. But it was small, and the CDC believed they could contain it, so we had reason to hope, and reason enough to largely ignore it.

Which is what I did, and more than gladly. I ignored it,

until I couldn't. And when I couldn't, that's when everything really started getting scary.

☼5☼
Comfort

I would like to digress here briefly and say that while pretty much everything that happened once the meteorite crashed into the city was bad, there were some good points about it as well. (Which makes it hard for me to completely regret everything; it *is* easier to regret something if nothing good comes out of it.) But still, I believed if it had never happened, things would have been much better off. Or at least more pleasant and convenient.

I returned to my right state of mind almost instantly after leaving the hospital. The reversion to the normalcy of everyday life was a relief for me. The panicky feeling I'd felt in the hospital was short lived, as the logic and reality of the outside world squashed any real concern to the back of my mind.

After all, if I was insane, logic stated, I would not be able to realize the absurdity of my thinking. Clouds, looking at me. Ha. Insane.

And reality stated that, since school was canceled, my time was better spent playing video games all day long at Jason's (without consulting my parents, of course), than worrying about being insane.

"Yes! I beat you again!" My bragging bounced off the walls. *Death Raiders III: Alien Slayer* was center stage for Monday's entertainment, as Jason and I battled it out.

I was feeling much better now that I was free of the hospital—so much so, that I believed the hospital was my source of insanity. I didn't know how Mark could work in one. It took a special kind of person, I supposed.

I personally looked forward to the day when I would become a lawyer like Cheryl, or maybe some type of political analyst for foreign countries. That sounded cool. I could travel then.

"You got lucky," Jason muttered as he angrily pushed the "restart" button. "Come on, this time I won't lose."

"I've beat you ten times already. Let's do something else," I complained, slightly irritated. *Doesn't Jason get that he isn't a challenge anymore, and therefore it's only half as fun to beat him?*

Sheesh. And I was the one in the hospital thinking *my* thinking was going down the tube. Looks like I at least had some to begin with. "Let's go outside and practice football or something."

"I don't really want to," Jason remarked. "It's getting colder, or haven't you noticed?"

Strange, I *hadn't* noticed. I had forgotten that it was getting closer to winter, and if anything, the past few days seemed warm to me. "All right, Jase, let's get some food. I'm hungry. Cheryl's goofy chef made egg whites substitutes and asparagus for breakfast today. That doesn't hold up after hours of playing video games."

Another annoying thing about Cheryl—she's constantly on a diet and doesn't believe in eating out unless business calls for it. I am the only person (well, guy, anyway) I know who remembers life in terms of diet periods. (This was the

"Veganite" period.)

"All right. I'll see if Mom has anything out in the kitchen. Just a warning, there isn't much since Friday's party." Jason put down his game controller, and I followed in suit.

"It smells funny in here," I announced as we walked into the kitchen. I noticed a pile of pizza boxes and sandwich wrappers from the doomed party still near the garbage can. "You going to throw those out before they rot?"

Jason huffed. "You can take them outside if you'd like, Dinger," he said as he opened the fridge. "Eh ... "

"What is it?" I asked, peeking over Jason's shoulder. "Ah, I see what you mean."

There was nothing in the large fridge but a half-empty jar of pickles, a slice of what appeared to be moldy cheese, and a blackened banana.

"So, you want to eat out?" I asked, reaching into my pockets. "I have some money on me."

"Well ... " Jason fumbled for words, and I briefly recalled Jason's lack of proper funding at the moment.

"My treat—since I beat you so many times at *Alien Slayer*." I smiled. "Come on. We'll have to walk, but there are a couple of places around here, right?"

Jason nodded. "All right. Sounds fair to me, since I let you win all those times."

"Yeah, sure you did. Oh, it looks like it's going to rain

79

gumdrops."

Jason's brow furrowed; he looked like he wanted to hit me for my comments, but realizing that would forfeit the free food, he merely asked, "Do you want to borrow a hoodie or something? It's chilly outside."

"Nah, I'm good." I waved off the request. "It's like summer to me. Where would you like to go?"

"Let's just go to Rachel's Café, okay? I don't think you've ever been there, but Rachel's really cool—and hot. She's getting married soon, I hear."

"Oh, really?"

Jason continued on as we headed out and down the street. "Yeah. She's twenty-three or twenty-four. Her boyfriend, Lee, is helping my dad get some freelance work right now."

"That … is interesting." Actually, I was quite bored. I just hoped the food was good.

A few blocks down and over, Jason nodded ahead just to the right. "It's right there, see?" He indicated a small place that looked more like a two-story house than a restaurant.

It was … okay, I supposed. But honestly, if Jason hadn't pointed it out to me, I'd have never noticed it. Even if I had, I wouldn't have gotten close to it without some pepper spray.

Walking into Rachel's Café, however, I liked it almost instantly. The decorations, menus, framed photos, and the paintings that hung cheerfully on the walls, while small tables and booths were cramped everywhere. It felt warm and welcoming and real.

"Yeah, it's cool here," Jason remarked, seeing my expression. "They have great food and music nights … uh, Dinger?"

I heard Jason beckoning me, but I ignored him. (Frankly, I just didn't like the idea of letting Jason think, even for a moment, that he'd ever be able to call the shots with me.)

I saw a painting by the door of a fiery bird, surrounded by dark starlight, reaching out its wings. Later, it would hit me how odd it was that I'd found quality art in a coffeehouse of all places. Usually those places were devoid of refined elements of culture.

"Uh, Dinger? Come on, you need to meet Rachel."

"Coming," I muttered, catching up at my own set pace.

"Hey there, Jason," a chipper voice called out in greeting. I assumed it came from the pretty redhead with gold-speckled eyes looking at us from behind the counter.

Wow. Jason was right (for once). Rachel, assuming that was Rachel, was absolutely gorgeous.

"Hi, Rachel." Jason nodded toward me. "This is my friend, Hamilton Dinger. He's never been here before."

Rachel's eyes lit up. (No doubt at the thought of a potential new customer.) "It's nice to meet you. I'm Rachel. And, if you haven't guessed, this is my café."

I returned the smile. It came easily enough. "I like it here.

81

You have a nice place."

"It's a small coffeehouse, but it houses big dreams. At least I think so." She giggled, instantly reminding me of an older version of Gwen. "Hey, would you guys like to try something new? I'm trying out a new recipe. It's an apple crumble, kind of like a tart-turnover pie."

"Sounds good," Jason replied. "I'll try it. Has Lee had it?"

Who's Lee? Oh, right—Lee was the guy Rachel was going to marry, and Jason was all upset about it and stuff … right.

"No, I just made them this afternoon," Rachel promised. "So you'll be the first." She hurried—practically skipped—off to the kitchen.

Jason grinned. "Always lots of perks here. Rachel's a good cook. You shouldn't have to worry about her food being off-tasting."

"Hey, I'll try it," I agreed eagerly. I was still hungry. And it *was* free food. (There is really no beating free food.)

A moment later, Rachel reappeared and handed us her treats. "So, Hamilton, was it? That's an odd name, if you don't mind my saying."

I cringed. My name has always been a more awkward part of my life. It has served its purpose of scarring me, driving me to be a successful, skillful, and charismatic individual—I never wanted to be an awkward person with an awkward name. On the bright side, it made me sound like a smart person. Not everyone can say that about their name (barely

THE STARLIGHT CHRONICLES

anyone can these days), and it was a good conversation starter.

"My mother's a lawyer. She has her undergrad in history. She was obsessed with Alexander Hamilton when she and my dad got me, or so they tell me," I said to Rachel. I had the lines memorized.

"*Got* you, Dinger? I didn't know you were adopted," Jason remarked with a laugh.

"I wish," I muttered. Although, thinking about it, those were the words my mother used, and my mother was a master of semantics.

Rachel laughed. "My mother was reading a romance novel when she was pregnant. That's how I got Rachel."

"Trust me, you have it much easier," I assured her.

The cowbell over the doorway clanked loudly, halting Rachel's bubbly giggles. I looked up to see a woman, who could only be Rachel's mother, walking in with a sour look on her face.

"Men are the stupidest things on the surface of Earth," she announced to the whole gala of people, before making her way towards the bar.

"We're not all bad, Letty!" an older man called out from the back, sending a fury of laughter fluttering through the crowd.

"Hi, Mom." Rachel waved. I wasn't sure, but there seemed to be some hesitancy behind her words.

From looking at the lady's grim face, it was easy to see she'd just had a disastrous date. Her graying hair was messy, and her (probably) once-nice dress was windblown. "Hi, Rachel," she greeted her brusquely before slumping down on a creaky chair.

"Bad date, I take it?" Rachel asked, getting a mug of strong coffee out for her mother.

I was bluntly amazed a woman like that could get a date at all.

Leticia—Letty—snorted. "You don't want to know." She shifted on the barstool and straightened out the wrinkles in her dress before sighing obnoxiously. "Oh, God! I used to be wealthy! But *no*, thanks to my brother and ex-husbands, I'm dashing around town in second-class clothing, living in the poor district like a welfare case, and going out on blind dates with men of the most insufferable kind!"

Huh. Dinner and a show.

Rachel gave her mother a sympathetic pat on the hand. "Don't worry so much, Mom," she said, putting on a bright smile. "You still have time to find a suitable date for my wedding."

"Ha," Letty huffed again. "Let me just say this, Rachel. You can count yourself very lucky, now that you've found yourself a half-decent man to marry. Nowadays, there aren't too many of those walking around." She dug into her expensive-looking knockoff purse and pulled out a cigarette. "If I had it my way, no man would walk at all."

84

I felt a sudden rush of gratitude for the American justice system.

"Mom, no smoking in here," Rachel reminded her. "And the doctor told you to stop. You already have high blood pressure."

"Life is pressure, darling," Letty sneered humorously, and that was when I first thought I might just like her enough to be amused. "Oh, why did I raise you to be so good?" she asked as she tossed her cigarette back into her purse.

"I'm sure you didn't mean to." Rachel laughed. "Here, I just tried a new recipe, and I want an honest opinion—and your opinion is as honest as they come, Mom." Rachel gave her an apple crumble tart before disappearing into the kitchen.

Letty took the tart somewhat reluctantly, but it calmed her down. (Food usually does that to overstressed women.)

"There you guys are," Rachel said to Jason and me kindly, handing us our orders. "I'm sorry for Mom …" she leaned down and whispered. "She's cranky today; she was up late last night helping my cousin."

"Is your cousin okay?" Jason asked. "Did the doctors figure out what was wrong with her?"

"No, but she's been under the weather for a while now," Rachel told him while I was busy concentrating on the food. That is until Letty distracted me, as she reached for some whiskey to add to her coffee.

Something timeless seemed to take hold of me. I glanced around the café again, and found myself admiring its various quirks. "I like it here," I decided aloud. "I'll come back." And as I said it, I knew it was true.

Rachel grinned; she wanted to hear that, I guess. "See that you do. We'll remember you, Hamilton. Right, Mom?" She glanced over just in time to foil another one of Letty's attempts to smoke.

Letty snorted and chucked her lighter across the room in reply, and I wisely swallowed a laugh at the sight.

She turned to Jason and me. "Don't you boys date until you've found a good-hearted woman to please, you hear? Else you'll be hearing from me, after I hear from Rachel."

We nodded as she picked up her clutch and headed out the door, coffee cup in hand.

As soon as she was out of sight, I shook my head. "It's a nice place, but there are some weird people here."

Jason sighed happily, peeking over at Rachel. "There's definitely something in the air."

Yeah, probably marijuana.

"So, how's business going, Rachel?" Jason asked, vying for all the attention he could get from his beloved barista. While I thought he was a bit on the pathetic side, I had to give him props for finding a girl who could whip up a mocha that was to die for.

"It's been growing, I think," she answered. "I've had a lot

86

of new customers today. I think it's because a lot of places nearby are closed for at least the week. Did you guys see any meteorite damage?"

"Yeah, sure did." I smiled proudly, about to recount to Rachel my heroic deeds.

She nodded to the television above us. "It's been on the news almost nonstop since it happened. The crash site's only a few blocks away from here. A lot of nearby buildings have been damaged. I guess we were lucky here. Nothing happened to us at all."

We looked around, with slight confusion, to see Rachel was telling the truth. In fact, if I hadn't known about the meteorite myself, coming in here, I would've never guessed it happened at all. "Strange."

"Well, a lot of strange things have been happening lately," Jason interjected. "I heard the meteorite blew up the other day when some guys tried to move it. They got a robot machine to move it to the science lab at Apollo City College."

Rachel nodded. "That's true. Lee's brother works there."

"You almost have to wonder if it's not really a bomb disguised as a meteorite or something," I replied thoughtfully.

Conspiracy theories make you sound cool, but only if you half believe them. If you get too excited, then people think you're nuts. Luckily, I mastered the technique years ago.

"It would explain why NASA didn't pick it up on radar," Jason agreed encouragingly. "Not until it was too late."

"Yes, it would." Rachel shrugged. "But seeing all the good that's come out of it for my restaurant, I can't help but think it's a miracle, almost."

"That's silly. It caused a lot of people to get hurt, and cost a lot of money in damages." I snorted disdainfully. "Plus, miracles don't happen. There's always a scientific explanation for stuff like this."

"It's sad you don't believe in miracles."

"Why?" I looked up at her with my best skeptical face ready. I loved arguing about this kind of stuff.

"Because, I suppose you don't believe in true love then." Rachel blushed. She put her hands up to her cheeks and sighed. Jason and I exchanged glances as Rachel went off into her girly daydream, and I knew, since Jason was her friend, I couldn't tell her what a ditz she sounded like. I settled for inwardly groaning.

True love, to me, was a nice term for the ignorant. In *my* opinion, true love could be reduced to a simple formula: How much money was involved (income and expenditures), and how willing a person was to communicate (also known as the X factor—motivation, is nearly impossible to predict). Of course, there were more anomalies involved (the Y— *"Why?!"*—factors), but those were the basics. People who believed in those "happily ever after" stories were doomed to find out they didn't really exist.

"Hey, Dinger, did you hear anything about the play?"

"Huh?" I looked up as Jason's off-subject question broke

THE STARLIGHT CHRONICLES

through my thoughts. "Oh, not really. I'm sure we'll find out when we go back to school." As if I even cared to know, recalling the bunny-faced Romeo.

"I hope it's still on," Rachel said, leaning over the counter. "It would really make the students of Rosemont happy."

"Rosemont? Why?"

Rachel replied, "Well, the art department of Rosemont Academy was working on the set. I heard the designs were beautiful."

"Personally, I think it's pointless. I mean, are you kidding me? *Romeo and Juliet?*" I snorted loudly, randomly thinking I did that a lot when I hated something. "All our plays almost always end up in a lawsuit over faulty staging equipment. Besides, Shakespeare died how many years ago? It's a rather awful story; Romeo's hysterical, and Juliet's a suicidal maniac."

"*Romeo and Juliet!*" the clanging of the cowbell at the door was accompanied by a loud, passionate, borderline senile, voice.

"Oh, no." Rachel grimaced, slapping her hand to her forehead.

We—everyone in the room—turned to see an old man standing in the doorway. He was thin as a rail, with a beard reminiscent of Santa Claus. The old man punched his fist into the air, and then began to recite:

"Two households, both alike in dignity, /

89

In fair Verona, where we lay our scene, /

From ancient grudge break to new mutiny, /

Where civil blood makes civil hands unclean. /

From forth the fatal loins of these two foes /

A pair of star-cross'd lovers take their life; /

Whole misadventured piteous overthrows /

Do with their death bury their parents' strife /

The fearful passage of their death-mark'd love /

And the continuance of their parents' rage /

Which, but their children's end, nought could remove /

Is now the two hours' traffic of our stage; /

The which if you with patient ears attend /

What here shall miss, our toil shall strive to mend."

With that, people cheered, and he took a very ostentatious bow.

"Oh, Grandpa," Rachel muttered as she shook her head, thoroughly humiliated.

I merely raised an eyebrow, hoping this guy was stable enough to be out in public, as he made his way through his adoring crowd. "That's your grandfather, Rachel?" And I thought my relatives were bad.

"Yes, unfortunately," she whispered. "Shh … here he comes."

"Ray, you know I have the hearing of a bat," her grandfather said. "There's no point in being secretive."

"I know. That's why I'm afraid."

The old man sat down next to me as Rachel filled his cup. "What are you doing?" he asked her. "Stop! I wanted coffee."

"You know the doctor told you to start drinking tea three times a day," Rachel shot back, still filling up the cup. "You can handle it, Grandpa, after making a show like that."

"You know I just do it to make you mad."

"You're insane," Rachel insisted, before hurrying back to the kitchen.

Deprived of his social victim, Rachel's grandpa turned his attention to me and Jason. "So, you boys in the play, huh?"

"No," we responded simultaneously.

"Shame … " he looked intently at me. "Such a wonderfully tragic story … much like your own story, huh, young man?"

I raised my eyebrows even higher than the last time. "What are you talking about?"

"Star-crossed lovers … " the old man whispered softly. "Stars-crossed … " Then he seemed to lose his train of thought. He took a sip of tea and bitterly swallowed it.

And then I was actually buying what he was selling, my

91

mind uncontrollably flashing back to the dream I had in the hospital. Stars … ?

No, I told myself. Stop. *He doesn't know anything about you. He's just unstable. Probably. And old.*

"Would you guys like a free dessert today?" Rachel asked us, probably as a pity gift. It's not every day you are sitting next to someone who might try to convince you toe floss is the next big thing.

"Really?" Jason's eyes lit up, and I completely understood why Jason was so much in love with Rachel. (Food usually does that, too.)

"Don't feed them poisoned apples, Rachel." Her grandfather chuckled into his tea cup.

"Ugh! You can have one too, Grandpa! It's perfectly safe. Besides, we were talking Shakespeare, not the Brothers Grimm." She handed us a plate full of dessert samplers. "Don't mind him. Grandpa Odd here used to be an English teacher. He's been obsessed with the stuff since my grandmother died twenty years ago."

Ah, so he *was* insane. The clarification helped.

"Wow, this is really good," Jason said, his mouth full of a dessert heralded as Rachel's Sweet Fruit Puffs. "Tastes like a pancake-pudding kind of combination."

"That's pretty close." Rachel smiled. "I hope you come back. Here's the bill." She handed us a sheet of paper and left to take care of her other guests.

We exchanged a telling glance; we didn't want to be caught alone with Grandpa Odd.

"Let's go, it's getting late," Jason said.

Nodding, I hurriedly pulled out the money while Jason grabbed his jacket.

"Hurry," I muttered. I was in such a rush that I barely noticed when I hit someone with the door on my way out. I thought the girl glared at me, but it was hard to tell for sure because a curtain of bangs hid her face. I ignored her more out of convenience than anything else.

"That old guy's so weird."

"I know," Jason agreed, as we started down the street. "I've only seen him a couple of times, but this is the first time I've ever heard him speak. Usually he sits there, quietly staring off into space. Still, Rachel's food is the best."

"Yeah, it was all good."

I groaned as the Apollo Time Tower, the city's oldest building and biggest clock, chimed four o'clock. "Ugh. I have to head home. Cheryl's supposed to be home soon. I hope that sandwich of Rachel's holds up until tomorrow." I made a face. "Estella-Louise is making organic vegetable stew tonight." My words were composed of only the purest of hatred for the grass clippings my mother's current chef had made for breakfast and was no doubt making for dinner.

Jason laughed. "Good luck with that one, Dinger."

"Ha, ha, ha." I laughed bitterly, as bitter as I was sure

dinner (assuming I ate it) was going to be.

☼6☼
Grievance

The meteorite blast had been one of the most exciting and frightening events the city had seen in years. It was sad to admit that, because it wasn't even that big. The news said it was close to twenty yards in diameter when it blasted through the atmosphere, but the biggest piece had significantly whittled away when it'd landed smack dab in the middle of Rosemont. Sure, people had gotten hurt and stuff, but really? That kind of stuff happens every day.

Part of the reason I didn't recognize the danger the meteorite's arrival presented was because I believed the danger was all over after it crashed. The other part was because I didn't care about it, except when it made me look really good—like the whole saving Gwen's life part.

Despite this, a big fuss went on practically all month about it—after all, something actually interesting going on was rare in Apollo City. (We usually lived vicariously through Cleveland, our sister city.) But thankfully, soon enough, everything seemed to be semi-back to normal.

That is, at least in school. True, the students were still quieter than usual, but it could just as easily have meant they had reverted to writing gossip on the bathroom walls again.

Probably the most inconvenient event was on Tuesday, when we got back to school the following week. We had to have an assembly. That wouldn't have even been that annoying, normally. After all, I get to hang out with my friends in the auditorium—talking and ragging on teachers,

95

unimportant students, and the like—while playing on my Game Pac.

It hadn't been a bad idea to get everyone together to goof off while we pretended it was for something important. But it had been a bad idea to get the librarian to help.

"Guys! Shh! Trixie alert!" I nodded to the far side of the row of seats, where our least favorite person in all the school suddenly appeared. It was the librarian, Ms. Brain, commonly referred to as "Trixie" by those who dared to seek her wrath.

Ms. Brain was definitely an ironic choice for a librarian. It wasn't really odd that she had extremely short, grayish hair (it was almost butch), with one strange curl in her bangs, or that she wore old-lady librarian shoes, which tapped the floor in an impatient, annoyed manner on a consistent basis. No, it was her voice that made her so ... unique. It cracked like a whip (an accurate comparison, too—it was often used as a weapon in the library). Poncey mimicked Trixie and Mrs. Smithe so well that if he was pushed into it, he could hold fake conversations between the two all on his own.

As my friends and I settled into our auditorium seats, we all felt the burn of her gaze. Trixie always glared down at us. We were a known group of "troublemakers," and have been ever since Simon decided mystery meat was an acceptable substitute for a football and tossed it around the cafeteria at some of the band geeks. It turned out that one of them, the one who ended up bawling like a baby, Kenneth Parker, just happened to have a mother on the school board and friends with Trixie.

So Trixie's black, old-lady librarian shoes rapped predictably, drumming irritation like a theme song. Even though she said nothing, I knew she was deliberate in her actions; she only wanted to intimidate us and assert her authority. Unfortunately, it was enough to effectively put a damper on my playtime.

"Ladies and gentlemen," Mr. Hinnish, Central's loveable and approachable, but scared, politically-correct principal, began, "The travesties of this past weekend have not gone unnoticed by any. I want to assure you no students in this district were significantly harmed ("Ugh!" I exclaimed angrily; my pain was nothing to these people, apparently), and no significant damage was done to this school. We are expected to have repairs completed today."

Mr. Hinnish went on to talk about the schedule for the week and other important-sounding stuff, like how *Romeo and Juliet* was still going on (though delayed), bringing cheers from some and groans from others. (I plead the fifth here.)

The best announcement by far was the next football game would be Friday night, Homecoming night, against the Clearburg Golden Tigers. That got students *really* cheering.

Believe me, there was nothing better than Friday night football at our high school—especially when it was the Homecoming game.

But even in the perfect teenage life of mine, I got bored easily.

Such as later, when I was sitting in drama class.

97

It was ninth period, and I felt my attention drooping as much as my eyelids. Mr. Lockard was droning on and on about Shakespeare and the Global Theater ...or was it Globe Theater? I wondered briefly how Gwen could lap this stuff up like cream. It left a dry taste on my tongue.

Had time passed at all since class began? I wondered. I dared not look up at the clock for fear Lockard would use it as an excuse to call on me.

I shifted in my seat. Immediately, I grimaced at the highly noticeable lack of legroom.

I sighed. Drama was the stupidest class ever. (Ironic I would think so, I know.) Gwen was the reason I'd signed up for it this year. Once she'd been assigned to another period, I made it my life's mission to drop the class.

Unfortunately, the parentals were not as keen on the idea. Mark and Cheryl made me keep it to "teach me a lesson" about suffering through things I detested. I still hated them for it. My parents would never understand how the anxiety produced in this class crippled my lifetime potential.

Not to mention my actual life was at risk while I was in the class. The drama room was located inconveniently (extremely inconveniently) underneath the stage. The wood-sanded ceiling-stage was composed of creaking boards only two inches thick. Two inches to keep people safe from falling onto unsuspecting students below, who were probably already half dead from boredom.

I was just waiting for the day when an amplifier, or microphone, or some fat kid caused the stage to collapse.

The humdrum of class slowly turned into muffles, which then twirled off into music. I was falling from consciousness, but not into sleep.

I panicked briefly for a moment as I fell back into the world of starlight, where I was flying freely, awing over the wonders of space and time Hubble had yet to find.

But even as I felt uneasy, I let myself be eased into contentedness. I wanted to enjoy it, even as I feared I was going crazy.

That same melody, the one from the hospital, called out to me, and I felt eagerness and euphoria, as though joy and anticipation had procreated an entirely new emotion within me.

My universe started to move with the music—as though the music had become not just sounds beautifully laced together, but a dance for all time and space to follow.

I couldn't help it when I laughed. Joy had tickled me, inside and out, so I laughed.

"Hamilton Dinger!"

My attention was roughly jolted back to reality as Mr. Lockard (loudly) called me out. The celestial background dropped from my eyes, as though a light switch had been flipped on, chasing away the warmth and protection of darkness, and I was faced with the white-hot exposure of Lockard's face.

"Just what is so funny?"

"Uh … " was the best response I could make. I had been laughing aloud, unintentionally. "Nothing."

"Then I don't want to hear *anything*." The unibrow on his forehead had an awkward, pointed slant to it.

I somewhat discretely rolled my eyes. Mr. Lockard knew full well drama was my least favorite class, somehow. I assumed he was used to students acting, and that made him more aware of when people were lying to him. That, or he was a mind-reading warlock. I was really fine with either explanation, as long as there was proof to back it up.

"Okay." Mr. Lockard clapped his hands. "As you all know, the play is going to be performed soon. Tomorrow we will be working on the set for *Romeo and Juliet*. I will also give extra credit for attending the play. Doesn't that sound wonderful, hem?"

How hilariously funny it would be to get Poncey to mimic Mr. Lockard, I thought. Lockard was a middle-aged, balding man with a bad comb-over and a unibrow, and had a tendency to say "hem" at the end of his questions instead of "hmm," or "yes," or nothing at all like a normal person.

Mr. Lockard, apparently using his dark magic for mind-reading, caught my eye. "Remember, drama is a good way to meet people. Don't you think so, Hamilton? I think it would be a nice way for you to meet a few more interesting ladies, hem?"

"Ugh, sure," I replied grumpily. As if I need help meeting girls. Lockard was an idiot. (I can't really stress that enough.)

I practically danced as the bell finally rang. Even math class was less depressing. I felt the layers of death-like sleep peel off me as I stepped out of the classroom. Happiness settled on me like an old friend, cloaking me with the music of my own universe.

I faltered slightly as it hit me. I'd been taken away, whisked off to the otherworldliness of my subconscious. If that's what it was.

I'd never had dreams before. Never. Not before the meteorite.

Was it possible my brain had been traumatized by my brush with death? Maybe I wasn't crazy, but something was physically wrong with me.

No. No, surely not.

Nothing was wrong with me. Nothing *could* be wrong with me. And even if there was, it wasn't my fault.

It wasn't my fault that I was surrounded all day long by idiots like Lockard, who insisted on boring me to death, while caging me under a forest of potential splinters, or sadists like Trixie and Lockard, whose sole ambition in life was to terrorize me.

It wasn't my fault I was born to be better than everyone else, but had to live with people who weren't worthy of me.

It wasn't my fault the meteorite had struck, slapping my city and branding me with bad dreams, either.

And it wasn't my fault I enjoyed the daydreams. Anything

101

to escape this life, really. I didn't have time to worry about them.

That's right. I didn't have time to worry about it. There were a lot more important things at hand to be concerned about. So I shrugged it off.

I was sure it was nothing, and that it would go away. So what if this one had happened while I was more or less awake? It didn't mean it was getting worse, necessarily. Lockard was just more boring than sleep, that's all. Surely I would be safe once I escaped his class. That was more or less how it'd worked with the hospital, right?

☼7☼
Distraction

As much as I said I wanted otherwise, it wasn't long before the dream world came to me again, letting me know in its own way it was determined to imprint itself firmly in my mind.

Friday's soft morning light slowly crept onto my bed, letting the day make her welcoming introduction. I heard the quiet echoes of the house calling out to me in my half-slumber, letting me know it was nearly time to get up.

I shook it off; a few more moments of uninterrupted sleep would be good for me. I'd been up late last night, looking over my history books and chatting online. Besides, I did not want to let go of my dreams just yet.

These were *real* dreams, I could tell, real dreams that mattered more than any fake or imagined dreams ever could.

I was dreaming about the Homecoming game. About scoring the last touchdown just as the last buzzer rang out. Endless people came pouring out from the stands, all coming to honor my game-winning catch.

And Gwen was there, too.

With my face in my pillow, still half asleep, a grin crawled up on my mouth.

I handed her the ball, and she leaned in. My smile grew as she moved in to kiss me, to brush her honeyed lips against mine in a tender, passionate embrace.

103

See? I told myself. Dreams you can control. Much better.

I leaned in to kiss Gwen back, determined to garner all the intentional happiness I deserved and desired.

Then she vanished. And so did everything else.

But a curtain of sleep remained, like the backdrop of the stars before.

"Huh?" I looked around. A flicker in the corner of my eye stole my attention.

A glowing star, growing steadily brighter.

"Come on, why now?!" I felt myself scream. Anger plunged through me, but my eyes wouldn't open into the real world. I was stuck.

I liked the dream I was having before; and even if the starlight dreams are nice, I'd still much rather dream about Gwen. "Stop it! I don't care about this! I don't want to see this. I don't want to experience this again!"

A noise squeaked up from behind me. I turned to see some people in the stands.

Okay, better than nothing, I thought, jogging over. "Hey!" I called, waving my arms, trying to get their attention.

No reaction.

I felt like an idiot as I walked up and placed my hand on one woman's shoulder. She had a strange, fixed gaze in her eyes. I was about to ask her what she was staring at when she suddenly fell over.

I fumbled to fix her before I looked at the others. They were all like that! Staring into space, looking at nothing. They were all … lifeless looking.

I was confused. I tried thinking of Gwen again. Tried hard. If I was going to have dreams, then I was going to be the one in charge of them.

But it was to no avail. I probably only made it worse.

A cold, creepy laugh splintered through the wind. Sudden pain sizzled down my back and around my right arm. "What is going on?!" I screamed, because now I was afraid. There was no controlling this.

And then mercy came as I woke up in bed, startled and breathing heavily, but alive and alone. "That was weird … " I looked down to see I was drenched in sweat. "Looks like I'm getting a shower this morning," I said ruefully. My arm was still stinging, causing me to question the reality of the situation once more.

Was I having a heart attack of some kind? Maybe a seizure?

I shook my head. If I wasn't careful, I was going to turn into one of those crazy people—what are they called? Oh, yeah. Hypochondriacs.

"Hamilton! Are you up yet?" Cheryl called up. "Breakfast is almost ready. Estella's just adding the finishing touches."

Perfect. I *was* going to be sick today.

But there was no way I could miss out on the Homecoming game. And staying home, or even going to the nurse, would kick me off that horse quickly enough.

I wondered if I had time to stop at a gas station or a fast-food restaurant to get *edible*, if not real, food before school started.

The whole school was abuzz with excitement as I arrived. With last week's game canceled, and all the other unsettling concerns, there was twice as much excitement for Homecoming as usual. Of course, more effort was usually required for decorating the building, organizing the parade floats, and getting all the other useless annual Homecoming contests ready, too. But there seemed to be a marked increase in the amount of energy in the school, so I decided not to be completely cynical about it.

During classes throughout the day, I found it hard to concentrate; I couldn't even seem to play Tetris. (A *really* bad sign.) It wasn't until ninth period that I started to feel better—if such a thing was possible in Lockard's class. I supposed, given the choice between flickers of my psychotic dreamland and deep, abiding hatred for drama class, I would rather focus on the latter.

Whoever said hatred was bad for you? Sometimes it is the only anchor you have keeping your world together.

THE STARLIGHT CHRONICLES

For drama, we were working on the stage today, and while it may be sturdier than it looks, I was not willing—or stupid enough—to go on faith alone.

The stage at least looked like a set for *Romeo and Juliet*, which, considering the limits on arts funding, said a lot about the effort of the volunteers. With a small house-like balcony, fake trees, and a couple of "ye olde doors," it was nice enough. I gave credit where credit was due.

Still not worth seeing, though. I'd rather study for the history exam. Or go to the dentist.

"Okay, students," Mr. Lockard called out. "Ten minutes left!"

I snorted. Even if this *was* Gwen's passion and soul, I didn't want anything to do with it.

"Hammy!"

Speaking of which—I smirked to see Gwen heading toward me. She must've come from her last class early. How … cute, I supposed. "Hi, Gwen."

She grinned back at me. "I didn't know you were in drama."

"Yeah, well. I figured I needed something that wasn't completely academic," I remarked. It's a safe enough comment with enough sting in it for me to still like it.

"Have you decided whether or not you're coming to the play?" she asked.

No safe comment there.

Maybe if someone dares me to, bets me to, or blackmails me to. "I'm still weighing the options," I replied ambiguously. And it was the truth, too. I was weighing the options of going to the play, gouging out my eyes, or going skydiving without a parachute. I was not sure which would be the best use of my time.

"I can't believe you're being so difficult about it." Gwen laughed teasingly.

"I don't know if I really want to see it. After all, we did watch the movie in last year's English class. Hardly worth it to go see the second-rate play version."

"Hey!" Gwen gave me an offended look and pouted.

"Second-rate play with only a first-class Juliet to boast," I added swiftly, beaming at her.

Ah, charm always works. Gwen immediately lost her confrontational air and melted at my praise, biased though it was. "So you'll come? For me?"

If it had been one of the guys, I'd have said I'd rather swim in a pool of spit than see Gwen kiss Tim, but her expression was so cheerful and happy and hopeful that I decided not to be cruel. I grinned. "What's in it for me?"

Gwen rolled her eyes and laughed. "Well, now that you mention it, a couple of the cast members were thinking about going out for ice cream after the performance on opening night. You could come with me, if you'd like."

I felt a rise of satisfaction brew inside of me. *That* was more like it. "Ice cream, huh?"

She smiled. "Tim and I wanted to go to Frosty's down on the east side of Shoreside Park. All our friends agreed that was a great choice. Do you like that place?"

The mention of Tim sent my satisfaction plummeting like an airplane out of gas. "Uh ... well, don't forget, the history exam is the day after," I said. "Can't be out too late."

"I'm in your class." Gwen sighed. "I know about it. Remember? That's me, in class, every day, just like you."

"Hey, Gwen! You came early, too?"

The instinct to retch at the sound of Tim Ryder's voice hit me hard. I really didn't like that guy.

"Hey, Tim." Gwen smiled shyly up at him. She waved and then turned back to me. "Hammy ... " She looked between us, clearly torn in some manner of thinking or another. Tim scuttled back when she turned away from him.

I smiled at her choice—because she'd chosen me, and that was the right decision. "Are you coming to the game tonight?"

Gwen's eyes glittered playfully. "What's in it for me?"

"You learn fast," I remarked with a laugh. "I don't know. Would you ... um, would you like to go somewhere after the game?"

"Maybe." Gwen gave me a small, teasing smile. "We'll have

to see if there's anything to celebrate."

"Of course there's something to celebrate. It's Homecoming, remember?" I smirked, confident. "We haven't lost Homecoming in twelve years. No way will we mess up this year."

"Hey, Dinger, what're you doing here?"

"Hey, Mike." I choked down a laugh as I saw Mikey. He was actually stumbling as he carried a large, wooden case. "Having some trouble there?"

"Shut up. It's heavier than I thought." Mikey shrugged. He leaned in a bit closer and said, "The girl carrying it was *tiny*. If you saw her, you'd never think she could carry it. Besides, at least I'm helping. You're not doing anything at all."

"I see you guys have become good friends again," Gwen spoke evenly, treading softly. All the school knew Mikey and I weren't always on the best of terms with one another.

"Mikey's like a brother to me." I shrugged. "Just because he's a little girl crazy and slightly backwards in his thinking, doesn't mean I'm going to abandon him."

Since Mikey had come to the hospital to see me, I decided graciously to forgive him for his stupidity. (Again.) Of course, knowing Mikey, it was bound to happen, but hopefully, he would learn one of these days that he wasn't humanity's prize.

"There's Courtney!" Mikey exclaimed, waving.

I looked back to see a tall, blond, and, objectively speaking, hot girl. So this was Courtney, I thought. I had to commend

Mikey on his choice if—and that was a big IF—she was able to string a coherent sentence together about something other than herself, music, or fashion trends.

"She's so cool! I just love her hair," Mikey gushed. Obviously, he was in his "obsession" phase.

I snorted disdainfully. "Well, that's the test of true love, I guess."

"Well, I've got to go," Gwen said. "I'll see you later, Hammy!"

"At the game, right?" I called after her. She just laughed in response, but it was enough for me to take it to mean yes.

Mikey grinned and poked me with his elbow. "So, you pulled the old 'saving her life' card?" He chuckled. "Looks like it worked. At least to the point where she's not sure she likes Tim much anymore."

"Really?" I looked skeptical. "She still talks about him at the wrong moments."

"Wrong moments?"

"Yeah, you know, when she's talking to me." I frowned.

"Oh." Mikey snickered. "Well, she's been kind of awkward around him lately. So maybe she's just waiting for you to make the move. Girls are too subtle sometimes, anyway. I would know after dating nearly all of them."

"Well, you know me," I replied. "I like to have them come to me."

"Just don't wait too long. Girls hate that, even if it does drive them crazy."

I huffed indignantly. "What did Courtney say when you asked her out?"

"I haven't asked her yet. You know me, Dinger. I like to have them come to me." Mikey grinned.

I laughed. There was a reason I was friends with Mikey.

☼<u>8</u>☼
Games

The buzzer sounded loudly over the roaring crowd. It was close to the end of the fourth quarter, with the Falcons winning by three points. The newly crowned Homecoming Queen, a senior girl named Brandi, screamed in support of her boyfriend, who was, of course, the Falcons' quarterback.

I was soaked with sweat as I jogged off the field. The Falcons were lucky so far this game. Upon arrival, we discovered the Clearburg Tigers had several Raider transfers from Rosemont on their team; no doubt that was careful planning by our old rivals. But despite the new additions, I just scored the Falcons' first and only touchdown in the whole game.

"Great catch, Dinger." Jason sat down beside me. "I guess I'm not going to play tonight." The half-hearted compliment was less cheerful than a doctor's appointment.

I smiled as I shrugged. "Sorry." I couldn't help that I was playing my best tonight. Jason, as my alternate, was just going to have to suck it up and deal with it. "Looks like Rosemont's been taking over Clearburg since their school was incinerated," I remarked, watching Poncey's struggle against an ex-Raider center twice his size.

"A lot of the Raiders went there, even though we're closer," Jason agreed as Simon was angrily tackled. "Ooh, that had to hurt. Simon will be black and blue tomorrow."

"Yikes." There was a lot of adrenaline in the Tigers/Raiders team tonight; their offense was more violent than ever.

113

Nearly twice as many fouls as usual had been called so far.

"No!" Jason screamed.

Looking up, I spewed water out of my mouth as the Tigers, fifteen yards away from the end zone, began to drive it home.

"Stop them!" I jumped up beside Jason. Both of us were yelling and cursing ferociously by the time our rival team scored.

The Tigers missed the field goal, thankfully, but there was still less than a minute for the Falcons to make a comeback.

"Offense, your turn! Show these guys what you're made of!" Coach Shinal called as the ref's time whistle was blown. I could tell by the tone of his voice he was tightly wound tonight; that was something, considering he's usually a very relaxed, easy-going guy. No doubt the Tiger converts were a surprise to him, too.

It seemed that the meteorite was once again causing me undue pain and suffering. It was going to be a hard game, and all things considered, Central could really use a win tonight. Morale had been lower than normal lately.

And my own morale tanked as I was putting down my water bottle. It was at that second that I felt it—the jolt in my chest. Something was happening. An image of horrid, evil, green eyes fluttered across my line of vision.

Okay. I had definitely been awake for that one. And I had either imagined it, or someone had managed to sneak hallucinogens into my water bottle.

Why did it only take the second between two of my heartbeats for my life to change so horribly?

"Dinger! You're up!" Coach Shinal called. "Go, get out there! What're you waiting for?"

For a quick second, I just looked at him. Was I imagining things? I felt my blood racing, my body temperature increasing. My right arm tingled in pain again, like something on fire had hit me. But Jason pushed me off the sidelines, and Coach Shinal shouted, "Come on, Dinger. We need you!"

I shook off the déjà-vu-like feeling as best I could. I hurried to my position, the right wing of the offense. Seconds later, the game was back on, along with all the pressure.

We *needed* this win. *Everyone* needed this win. Especially after two weeks with endless hours of news coverage on the devastation of the meteorite, the plague of worry unleashed upon my city, and my own personal hell of indecipherable, incomprehensible daydreams, which threw me into a whirlwind of simultaneous contentment and confusion.

Okay, so maybe *I* needed this win. But I deserved it.

The Tigers kicked off, and the ball headed down the field.

Greg Wilson, our quarterback, grabbed it straight out of the air and took off. All the Falcon banners waved eagerly as he started to run as fast and as cleverly as he could. I hurried after him, in case I needed to tackle someone.

Fifteen seconds were left in the game.

The crowd stood up, cheering as the band struck up an

energetic tune, and the cheerleaders hopped up and down, waving their pompoms like crazy. Everyone was so full of hope. I grinned to myself. Greg was gaining yards, hurdling down the field like lightning. It wasn't hard to believe we were about to win.

A second later, the Clearburg defense rushed in. Greg skidded to a halt, hurried to the left, faked right. He dodged the main line of defense, only twenty yards away from a touchdown.

"Go, Greg!" Queen Brandi yelled down the field to her boyfriend.

So close! Fifteen yards left.

Greg had just reached the ten yard line when a Rosemont-turned-Clearburg defensive player knocked him down to the ground. But thankfully, Greg, who was just as good a player as me most of the time, managed to hang onto the ball.

A whistle was blown. Time out.

Ten yards and eight seconds remained.

"We can do this!" I yelled excitedly, joining the team huddle.

"Yeah," Greg agreed. "We've got time. We've got strength. We've got smarts. We only have time for one play, so let's make it a good one. Bring home the glory! Run play Alpha-22. Ready, break!"

"Break!" the rest of the guys shouted.

Play Alpha-22. I smirked. I knew what to do.

As Greg cried out, "Ready, 42. 22. Hike!" I felt a rush of cold wind, energizing me even as it slowed me down.

I'd just reached the end zone when light flashed before my eyes again. My hands flew up to my eyes, but my helmet blocked me from rubbing them clear.

It was then the onslaught of terrified screams began.

"No, please! Help!"

"Police, help!"

"Augh!"

I gave up trying to block it all out. I stopped running and awkwardly looked around.

A man in black caught my attention. Not only had he concealed his face and body, but he had an awkward gait, like he'd stepped on something and it was causing him pain. I felt a rush of recognition as my arm sizzled with nerve-firing pain.

A name dripped through my body, but my mind wasn't able to interpret it.

The man was just leaving the stands when I noticed all the people in his path were not moving, and they had lost expressions on their faces.

Just like my dream! Alarm sputtered inside of me, and I looked for a referee or someone who could help when—

Smack! The football hit me. Right in the head. Right before it bounced off and went flying.

I tumbled over and recoiled, both in surprise and in pain, as the whole Falcon side went crazy with rage, while the buzzer buzzed and Clearburg fans cheered.

I looked over to see the ball five feet away from me, lying innocently on the ground. "Ugh," I groaned. I didn't need half a stadium of people booing to know this wasn't the happy ending we wanted.

"What went wrong, Dinger?" Jason asked, as his face suddenly appeared, hovering over mine.

Greg was complaining loudly; I could hear him even through my helmet. "I threw it right to you, Dinger! I can't believe you missed it!"

"Hey, lay off, Wilson!" Mikey yelled, shoving back our ticked-off quarterback. "Dinger still scored more in this game than you did! What were you doing, making googly-eyes at Brandi?!"

Greg shoved back as I watched, blank faced. A small scuffle ensued until Coach Shinal showed up. "Stop it! Go congratulate the other team." His lips were tight and his face was ashen white. We had good reason to listen.

The guys clearly wanted to complain some more, but they reluctantly headed over to slap hands with the Tigers. I started to follow, but I stopped short as I remembered. "Guys, we've got to go help! Those people need help!"

Jason turned on me. "Are you crazy? *You're* the one who needs help! If you were going to fail, you should've let me play!"

"Jase, come on," Mikey interjected. "Even Dinger's allowed to make mistakes occasionally."

I lost my resolve as despair clutched at my chest. For the first time in twelve years, Apollo Central had lost a Homecoming game. And it was all my fault! I was so upset I barely even noticed the sound of ambulances in the background.

As I walked into the locker room, I briefly glanced back in the direction of where the star had been in my dream. I saw nothing there.

"You think Dinger's gone off the deep end?"

"I think he missed it purely on stupidity."

"Maybe he was tripping or something."

"Yeah, maybe tripping on *drugs*."

"Shh, shh … there he is."

As I walked into the room, half the team quieted down, while the other half started throwing out insults.

"The pass was perfect! Didn't you *want* to win?"

Simon even came over and spit out, "We're not going to get into the playoffs because we lost tonight. Thanks a bunch!"

"We lost the first Homecoming game in twelve years because of you!"

"That's enough!" I shouted. "The reason I missed the ball, the *real* reason why, is because there were people in the audience who needed help!"

"Yeah, they probably needed help after you missed the ball, Dinger."

I frowned. "No, they were being attacked!"

"Hey!" Coach Shinal appeared with a scowl on his face. "None of that. We share both blame and glory when it comes to football." He patted me on the shoulder. "Good work tonight, Dinger," he said.

I knew he was just being nice.

Coach Shinal cleared his throat. "Good game tonight, boys," he started out. Everyone looked at him like he had suddenly broken out into song. "I am proud of all of you. I didn't know Rosemont's team members were playing with the Tigers tonight. We could've been better informed, but we hardly could've been better prepared. See you Monday for practice. Now go home."

The team nodded glumly in response.

Coach Shinal added, "Those alluding to the idea Dinger is the one to blame for our loss should apologize before leaving."

The team grumbled, but did as they were told. An indistinguishable choir of apologies was mumbled out in my general direction.

As we were leaving, the coach added, "And just to set the record straight, Hamilton was right. Close to thirty people were carted off in ambulances tonight so far, as I've heard."

☼2☼
Dreariness

Sleep eluded me half of the time over the next few days, and the other half of the time it plagued me with dreams of a nightmarish sort. It must've been in cahoots with the rain, which started pummeling the ground shortly after my nightmares came, and stayed long after I'd woken up silently screaming, several nights in a row.

During those nights, while I was wide-eyed with fearful restlessness, I wondered if the nightmares came because of my failure at the football game.

They were terrifyingly vivid, even days later.

The first one especially.

I felt curious, eager, and shocked silent and still, while the man in black I'd seen at the football game—I called him Orpheus, certain that it was his name, though I was just as certain I'd never met him—poured his own silver-light of soul blood out onto seven glowing crystals. The mix of lights was like fire made of many flames, glimmering with pride, energy, and excitement.

I knew they belonged to those in the crowd now rendered soulless.

The terror of familiarity hit me as the crystals glowed, giving birth to seven warriors as the light poured over them—Orpheus' band of women warriors, all lovely but deadly.

THE STARLIGHT CHRONICLES

The feeling of hatred and jealousy for the man himself froze me, capturing my attention like a slow-motion car wreck; awful, but I couldn't look away. I could not free my gaze from his face as he laughed.

Confusion swirled, puddling through my cloudy thoughts, each naming a crystalline warrior, too colorfully absurd to be real. Asteropy, Taygetay, Meropae, Maia. Elektra, Celaena, and Alcyonë. Names that whisper of a different time, a different place, a different purpose. A different life.

They all glimmered with a curse, with restraint, and I was relieved about that. Somewhat.

I looked expectantly for another face, but did not find it. Then suddenly more emotions poured through me, and I could not stop them.

Desperation. Anger. Hatred. Revenge. It all pumped through me, more than just a sensation or desire; it was a full-blown life force. It punched me out of sleep into awareness, leaving me weary, even as power charged through my veins.

No wonder sleep left me for hours after that dream. I'd walked into my dreams with some sort of Shakespearean death wish, and a tsunami of adrenaline had washed over me. Those faces were as real as my own, as though I were watching the secret unfolding of the end of the universe. The rain still wasn't helping, either; it howled and hounded me, like a warning, like an unwelcome wake-up call.

But my terror at the truth of these things was only as strong as my denial of it.

The second dream I had was less frightening, but more confusing.

In it, there was a shadow. I knew it was a girl, but I had never met her—or so I thought. I couldn't see her face, really; she was a silhouette leaning against the side of a brick building—one I recognized, but couldn't seem to place. She was standing out in the rain as I watched her, the same rain that had pulsated through the skies all week.

I saw her look up, and I mimicked her gaze, blinking away the globbing droplets of rain.

I heard her whisper something, but my mind only caught muffles. Something about clouds, I thought, but I wasn't sure.

Then she looked down at her wrist, and on the underside of her arm, there was a glow that startled me. Eerie and ominous, she glowed as the rain spiked down on her. I remembered taking a step closer, and seeing her hair darkened by the dampening water.

A shadow hung over her eyes, but I seemed to know they were watching me.

Then I heard her words, clearly this time.

"It's about time. I was beginning to wonder." The words were spoken with mild relief, but there was much more feeling hidden behind them.

Then the Apollo Time Tower rang, and I woke up to find my alarm clock screaming bloody hell at me, the sky cackling with lightning and thunder.

"Hey, Dinger!"

I have a headache. And possibly a stomach ache, too, though I am not sure if it had been brought on by Estella-Louise's cooking or the recent near-sleepless nights I'd had. So, *of course*, Poncey would annoy me endlessly today. Today, while I try with every ounce of brain power I had to find a way out of believing myself to be either sick or mentally ill. (Neither were really good options.)

I guess the distraction was welcoming because I actually responded. "Hey Poncey," I said as he sat down at his desk.

"Nice day out, huh?" Evan grinned, but the rest of the guys in my inner circle sighed. The city streets had quickly become devoid of people this morning. The few who were out were rightly huddled under umbrellas or hooded jackets, taking what cover they could from the piercing raindrops. Meteorologists had mentioned on the news this morning that they had no clue where the storm of the last few days had come from, but they were considerate enough (this time) to admit their radar systems could be on the fritz.

I was just glad none of the guys on the team had said anything about the Homecoming game this week. I was also glad most of them had properly resumed their hero worship

125

of me quickly enough, despite being lazy about it.

Coach Shinal was in a bad mood this week though. So were a lot of other adults. Even Martha, I had noticed, for all her coffee inhaling, needed a good nap. Her baggy eyes were mostly hidden by her glasses, but her frown was extra droopy and extra cranky today.

"Ugh, I can't believe this!" Drew slumped over at his desk, his head hitting the surface with a *bang!* He grimaced. "Man, it even hurts to goof off today," he muttered.

"When it rains, it pours," Poncey quipped.

Jason nodded, sleepy-looking. "I wish I could just stay home and do nothing," he agreed. "My body's not prepared for school today."

"Yeah, it's usually your mind that's unprepared." Poncey grinned. He appeared to be the only one of us who was excited, or at least somewhat energetic. "I wish—"

"Shut up, Poncey." The rest of us groaned.

"Where did the sun go? On a coffee break?" Jason grumbled.

"Looks like another day of review in here, too," Drew muttered, his eyes fastened on Martha as she wrote on the board. "Man, history's the hardest class ever. I looked at the test's study guide yesterday during third period. Nearly collapsed looking at everything we have to know. Mr. Gallows almost had a heart attack when I freaked out over it. He was like this"—Drew made a wide-eyed, gasping expression—"and only calmed down after he made certain I wasn't choking."

I nodded. "Mr. G's a good guy. He'd likely call the ambulance if you scared him enough."

"Getting me an ambulance doesn't help me much right now. Maybe later … I don't know how you manage it, Dinger. Top marks every time. I wish I had that kind of luck."

"It's something you're born with, sorry." I easily dismissed the notion as I pulled out my Game Pac. I'd flipped through the history book a few times since the weekend, but that was it. The exam was on Friday, so I didn't really care. I had other things to worry about.

Like trying not to think about how I was slipping on the edges of the cliffs of insanity. And winning my Tetris game.

Ah, it was nice concentrating on getting all the pieces of the dropping puzzle to fit together. The rhythm of the game enthralled me. I paid no mind at all to Martha as she started on with her usual lecture. It was the week before the big test, and everybody else was furiously copying down notes. I was in my own preferred world, where I was Tetris King, and there was no one else. No faces, no duties, no hard-pressed psychotic illusions to deal with.

It was good to see things were getting back to normal at last. Nothing ever went wrong when things were normal. (Or least, nothing went wrong to where I couldn't talk myself out of it.)

"Okay, class. Let's talk about chapter five—" Martha suddenly stopped talking and began tapping her foot. It was at this cue I looked up and grinned as harmlessly I could. As I expected, she was staring down her nose at me again, frowning.

"Dinger, are you going to be playing games all through my class today?" she asked exasperatedly.

"Sorry, Martha—er, Mrs. Smithe. Force of habit," I harmlessly explained.

"Put it away, if you want to keep it." There was a slight sharpness to her voice, and I was surprised to see that she was not kidding around today. Weird, usually she was a lot nicer about being mean, especially on the first time she called me out. "Let's get on with chapter five."

"Ah, come on, Mrs. Smithe," Poncey squawked up. "We went over chapter five last time. We know it already."

Mrs. Smithe turned her angry glare to Poncey. A few snickers were heard on the other side of the classroom at Poncey's assertion. I noticed Gwen wasn't laughing, but Brittany and her friends were trying (somewhat) not to giggle.

"Fair enough," Mrs. Smithe said, surprising me and probably the rest of us who were smart enough to catch it. "Instead of playing a review game for class, you are all going to study on your own. And if you aren't studying," she warned, "I'll give you a detention."

She then walked over to her desk and sat down. "Well? Why aren't all of you studying?"

128

THE STARLIGHT CHRONICLES

The class was just gawking at her, I noticed, waiting for the punch line. When she stared back at us, a few of us moved to get our notes out. Others began complaining.

"No way. Come on, Mrs. Smithe—"

"We have to suffer because of Evan? That's not fair!"

"Way to go, Poncey!"

"Yeah, why don't you just keep your fat mouth shut from now on?"

There were many complaints made, but Martha glared at everyone. "Class, studying requires *silence*. You have the rest of the period to *silently* study on your own. Now get to work."

The grumbles didn't stop, but they did become more muffled. I looked over at Gwen again; she wasn't happy. And she wasn't the only one. Brittany's giggles had disappeared, and there was a murderous gleam in her eye as she glared at Poncey.

"It would be so funny if they got together," I muttered to myself as I began to play Tetris again. I knew I was disobeying Martha, but I didn't think she would actually do anything. She'd probably just grade papers, or read a book, or something else teacher-ish.

And I was right. Mrs. Smithe just sat there, at her desk, grading papers and drinking coffee. And she did that throughout the period.

"Psst! Dinger!"

THE STARLIGHT CHRONICLES

"What is it, Poncey?" I asked, never looking up from my Tetris game.

"I'm beating you!"

I paused here, mostly because of the unlikelihood of the matter. Poncey had his own Game Pac out. "Poncey, you only have fifteen thousand points." I observed. "My high score is thirty-three thousand, remember? Amateur."

Some of the guys nearby who were looking over their notes and/or scanning their textbooks laughed.

I turned back to my game, where I was on the fifteenth level, with a total of ten thousand points. I might've been behind Poncey at the start, but it wouldn't take Poncey long to screw up. Or I would just surpass him anyway.

"Oh, hey, Mrs. Smithe," Poncey said in a sheepish tone.

Ha! Poncey's not going to fool me with that trick again, I thought, recalling Poncey's one stroke of genius at Jason's party.

But a moment later, a shadow came over me and I inwardly grimaced.

A sloshing feeling was whirling in my stomach again as I looked up.

Oh, crap.

"Ha! I can't believe you finally got a detention!" Mikey exclaimed as he met up with me in the hallway after eighth period.

"Shut up, Mikey," I muttered warningly. "I'm going to get Martha to take it away."

"Yeah, good luck with that," Mikey sputtered as he just laughed harder.

My expression turned sour. "You know, I'd expect you to be just a bit more careful around me, considering you upset me *last* week."

"That was last week? Wow, I thought it was more recent than that," he joked. "Sorry. But hey, we'll be in detention together at least."

"Oh ... that's right, you've still got all those detentions from Ms. Nolte, huh?"

"Of course. It's been more than a week, and she still can't look me in the eye. That's reward enough for me."

"Biology isn't hard," I remarked. "Why don't you just pay attention?"

"I just don't want to be here," Mikey told me. "I want to ... I don't know. I just want to get out of here. School's never been my forte, like it's been yours."

"Well, I don't like school work either," I said, which was true. "But that doesn't mean I intentionally suck at it."

"Well ... we're all unique."

131

"That's a lame excuse. You just don't want to work hard. Lazy."

"Well, I want to play football one day. What do I need science for?" Mikey asked as he started to head off for last period. "I'll see you in detention later—with Mr. Lockard!"

"I'm not taking it, remember?"

"Sure, sure … we'll see." Mikey laughed once more while I seriously considered punching him.

"We'll see indeed," I muttered. In fact, I thought, I will go and take care of it right now. That way I wouldn't have to worry about it later. What's wrong with taking time out of last period anyway? It's just stupid drama, and Mr. Lockard was probably busy with last-minute details for the play. He wouldn't care (or notice) if I was there or not.

"Hi Mrs. Smithe." I put on the goody two-shoes face as I walked into her classroom.

"I'm not going to take your detention away, Dinger, before you start spouting out your apologies or "reasonable" excuses and whatnot."

She'd obviously prepared for this.

"I wasn't going to ask you to take my detention away. I was going to thank you, actually," I began, still smiling, though my resolve has ebbed. "I've realized that I've become very lackadaisical in my work and in my studies lately, and I guess a lot of it has to do with stress and Friday night's game."

I thought maybe this was where I should've broken down

132

into tears, but I wasn't sure Mrs. Smithe would have bought it so soon.

"Dinger, you know if you're having problems, you should see a tutor. Or a doctor, depending."

"I know," I said. "It's not really schoolwork giving me trouble."

"Well, you're certainly getting into more trouble in school, if not in your schoolwork," Mrs. Smithe responded as she took a drink from her coffee container. "We've been back in school for over two months now, Dinger."

I grinned. "Well, I did realize my shortcomings. And I have a solution. So what do you say we forget the detention, since at this point, it's not very necessary?"

Mrs. Smithe shook her head and smiled pleasantly. (Her first all week, probably.) "I knew you were faking it." She laughed. "I might not see everything under the sun, Dinger, but I catch on pretty quick. Do you need a pass for next period?"

"Ah, come on, Mrs. Smithe." I sighed. "I'll make a deal with you—don't give me detention, and I won't play Tetris in your class again, I promise."

"How about this?" Mrs. Smithe got up from her seat and walked over to the door. "You don't play Tetris in my class, and you won't have to sit through another detention. Now, do you need a pass to get to next period or not?"

I must've stood there, dumbstruck, for several moments

before answering her question. "Yeah, you better give me one." I nodded grumpily. Angry as I was, I knew it wouldn't be smart to push the issue. Besides, my dignity had already taken a few hits during the conversation. "Mr. Lockard doesn't like it when I'm late. He already hates me because I didn't want to be in his stupid play."

"Mr. Lockard, the drama teacher?" she asked. "He definitely has his favorites, all right. Why didn't you want to be in the play, Dinger? Chances are you'd make a good actor. You certainly have no problem with memorization, and you would love the attention."

"I have more important things to do." I shrugged. "I don't really care."

"Aren't any of your friends in the play?"

"Oh, yeah. But just Gwen, really. She's Juliet."

"Gwen Kessler? Oh, she's such a sweetheart."

"Yeah. She took Mr. Lockard's intro class last year and a workshop of his at the Apollo City Theater during the summer. It's not a real surprise that he chose her," I murmured.

"She'll look really good next to that nice Tim Ryder fellow who's playing Romeo."

"Yeah, whatever." I rolled my eyes. My back was to Mrs. Smithe, so I didn't really care if she heard me or not. "Well, better go." It's going to be a long class, and an even longer detention, I thought bitterly.

☼10☼
Detainment

After the first ten or fifteen minutes, I completely understood why detention was a horrible punishment—I'd gotten stuck talking with Samantha Carter, a living gossip column.

I'd met Samantha on the swim team last year (and regretted it ever since). I supposed she was pretty enough to be kept out of the ugly house, as long as she kept clean. She was Juliet's nurse in the play, and despite her "involved" role, she'd subjected me to her constant blathering since I arrived.

"What do you think, Hamilton?"

"Huh?" I saw she was looking at me intently. I hadn't paid any attention to her babble in the least. "Oh … I completely agree with you." I hoped this sentiment was vague enough to work.

Apparently it was. Samantha smiled. "If you want to, there's a poll going around; it's five dollars for your first bet. I'm betting Tim and Gwen will get together on opening night! Can you imagine? It's just so romantic!"

I groaned. That's what she'd been talking about? No wonder I wasn't listening. I saw Gwen come into the auditorium. "I have to talk to Gwen!" I said hurriedly. I just hoped my desperation didn't crack my voice.

"Hey, no cheating!" Samantha called after me.

"Hey, Hammy. What's wrong?" Gwen asked, seeing my

136

peeved expression.

"That girl's nuts," I whispered, glancing over in Samantha's direction. "Please, Gwen ... help me out of here."

"You mean Samantha Carter?"

"Yes!"

"She's nice."

"Nice? Try annoying."

Gwen giggled, making me an interesting mix of angry and happy. "Go wait for the Rosemont students coming today; they'll need some help unloading the van when it arrives. That'll keep Sam out of your hair. She's working on costumes today."

"Sounds great." I'd do anything to get away from the chatterbox of doom—including helping out Rosemont students.

"Mikey usually does that, too," Gwen added. "So you can wait for him if you want."

I grinned approvingly. "Thanks. This means a lot to me."

"It's nice to know I can help you. I don't think I've ever had to before."

"Hopefully you won't ever have to again," I remarked, placing my hand on her shoulder affectionately.

"You know, it won't kill you to let others help you," she said wryly.

"I know. That's what I've got Simon and Poncey and Jason for."

Gwen rolled her eyes. "I didn't mean by switching homework."

"People! People!" Mr. Lockard clapped his hands as he walked up on stage. "Shh!" Everyone looked up at him as he primly straightened up. "Welcome, all. Today, we will finish up the set. So make sure to get your new friends' digits before you leave if you like them—and if you don't, well ... hem."

Mr. Lockard continued on, mentioning some other important-ish-sounding stuff, laced with some attempts at humor, spurred on only by the giggly girls in his audience who were probably laughing at him, not with him. (Unless they were suck-ups, of course.)

I felt like laughing or gagging or both. Adults who tried to be cool were *so* uncool.

"Uh, Dinger ... move!"

I inwardly retched. Brittany Taylor was the stage manager, a.k.a. the looming shadow over my head for that moment. Of course she wouldn't pass up a chance to legitimately harass me for the next hour.

"You know I'm leaving after the detention bell rings," I reminded her.

"I'll remember that, so I can boss you around as much as possible then." Brittany disliked anyone connected with Poncey. It was a well-known fact.

138

Another predictable side-effect of being popular—you have to take sides occasionally. This is best done with careful logic and diplomatic but decisive execution. And ever since Evan humiliated Brittany years ago at a group party by refusing to kiss her (it was a truth-or-dare dare, and I had to take his side; I wouldn't have wanted to kiss her either), she'd been out to bury him.

Only socially, of course. I think.

I walked away from her anyway. No need to increase my chances of becoming a victim of her wrath.

"Hey there, Dinger," Mikey greeted me. "Whoa, you're having a bad day. Imagine how much worse it'll be when you tell your parents you got detention today."

My mouth dropped open. Very few people ever blatantly made me angry. "Why are you so cruel today?"

"To make up for Friday's game." Mikey grinned. "Come on, I'm kidding. Follow me. We'll be safe from Ms. Sour-puss-in-her-pants outside. Unloading the Rosemont-mobile is the funnest job you can have here."

"'Funnest' is not a word."

"But you get to listen to the girls' gossip going around backstage while you wait."

"I'm sure you like that, but believe me, I've heard enough gossip for today," I said, recalling Samantha's insights into the shallow world of gossip girl. I looked outside and saw it raining harder than ever. Appropriate.

"Man, is this rain ever going to stop?" Mikey complained. He spotted a large bus on the road. "There they are! I can smell Courtney from here."

"That's not disturbing at all." I turned to roll my eyes, and that was when I saw Poncey coming up behind us. "You're late."

I wasn't the only one who'd received a detention from Mrs. Smithe.

Poncey smiled. "What Lockard doesn't know won't kill him … unless it's something that's supposed to kill him."

"Like a haircut?" I joked.

Poncey snickered. We both knew Lockard was never going to get one those; not with that comb-over.

The rain pummeled down on us like blunt needles as we hurried outside to the vehicle. A pretty, but cranky voice called out, "Mikey, are you going to get my stuff or not?"

The voice belonged to a tall, blonde girl with enough makeup on her face to paint a wall. I looked at her and decided she could probably tell someone how to voluntarily throw up, too. It was nice to see Courtney again.

I struggled to keep a laugh down as Mikey, in the middle of hoisting a box over his shoulder, received his sweetheart's first reprimand of the day.

"I'm coming, Courtney," Mikey told her. "Just wanted get this in."

"It's only *my* stuff you're supposed to get." Courtney huffed angrily. "Put *that* stuff down and help me unload my paints!"

Whoa, I thought. Somebody woke up on the wrong side of the cave this morning. What a bear.

I felt a twinge of pity for Mikey, who put the box down immediately and then hurried off to serve Lady Bear. She might've been pretty, but I wouldn't go within ten feet of her, not even to save my life.

I poked Mikey, and nodded to the wooden case he'd just put down. "That's the one you couldn't hold onto before."

Mikey sighed. "You take it. I have to grab Courtney's stuff." One of Mikey's better traits was that he tended to be quite loyal in the beginning of a relationship. I would've felt sorry for him if it hadn't been his own fault.

I grinned, but when I picked it up a moment later, I was surprised. It *was* heavy. I gruntingly took it inside and put it down near the door. I couldn't resist a smirk in Mikey's direction on my way back out.

A few moments later, Mikey and I finished dragging a number of supplies and boxes up to the stage.

"Ha! I told you." I grinned at Mikey.

Mikey laughed. "Yeah, sure. You're going to be wrong about something one of these days. Or you're going to pay for proving me wrong."

Back in junior high school, it was the general opinion that Poncey was more like my fool, while Mikey was more like my brother—mostly because he got away with arguing with me several times and did not usually suffer some sort of physical or social punishment for it.

I like to think we've matured somewhat since then.

"Do I even want to know?" Gwen reappeared, laughing as Poncey came shuffling around the corner with bags draped over his back.

"Dinger bet me we could carry all this stuff up here in one trip," Mikey explained, poking the accusing finger at me.

"That's everything. Thanks, guys." Tim came up and started to put his arm around Gwen's shoulders, but quickly stopped when he saw me. "Hey, Dinger."

I smirked. "Hey there, Tim."

Tim laughed awkwardly, probably glad I didn't make him uncomfortable. (Not for a lack of desire on my part.) "Gwen, let's take this stuff to its rightful owners."

"Sure, good idea." Gwen grabbed a couple of bags we'd just put down before heading off with Tim. I followed with Mikey at a slower pace. (We had more bags and boxes, Tim being a pansy boy and all.)

"Hey, Tim," I heard Gwen ask, "Do you hang out with

Hammy and his friends at all?"

"Not really," he admitted. "Dinger doesn't like me."

[Insert sarcastic clapping here]. *Well said, Tim, well said.* I couldn't agree more. I had to snicker. Obviously, Gwen and Tim didn't notice I was a mere eight steps behind them.

"What? Why not?"

"Well ... he likes you." Instantly I felt my blood start to boil. If only Gwen wasn't around. Tim was not worthy of confessing my feelings.

"Huh? No way." Gwen shook her head, and then I was even more enraged than before. I'd kill him, I decided. Or I would let him die by omission. Whatever came first.

"I'm serious, Gwen," Tim said. "Guys can always tell when another guy likes a girl. And he likes you. So he hates me. Simple relationship politics."

"He doesn't hate you. Why would he?"

Oh, I hate him, all right. There would be no redemption for him after this.

"Yes, he does. I, well ... I like you." Immediately Tim turned a shade of red that made me think of a bursting thermometer.

Gwen was as shocked as I was appalled. "You mean ... you like me?"

He blushed again. "Well, yeah."

143

As the two of them reached the bottom of the steps, Mikey apparently decided I'd had enough. (Poncey was taking a short break while his back realigned.) He clapped me on the shoulder. "Move it."

I struggled against him for a moment, but Mikey pulled me off to the side of the rounded staircase, where I could still watch and hear but not be seen.

"You mean in that way?" Gwen had an incredulous look on her face.

"Yes." Tim exclaimed. "Yes, I like you that way! I've been trying to tell you for a while now but after Jason's party, I didn't think I was good enough for you, and everyone else seemed to think the same."

Gwen was silent for a moment before she reached out and took hold of Tim's hand. "Please, don't be scared, Tim." she smiled kindly.

I felt my stomach churning as Tim peeked over at her and asked, "Do you like me, too, Gwen?"

Under any other circumstances, I would've laughed. Tim's voice cracked and the skin on his face had turned a tomato red. (The pimples stood out like white pockmarks.) But as Gwen smiled and started to reply, all the things I suddenly felt like doing involved blood. Blood and vomit.

I didn't mind when she was interrupted.

"Okay. People, people!" Mr. Lockard was center stage once more, waving his hands all around, demanding attention.

THE STARLIGHT CHRONICLES

"Get a move on, hem?"

I shuffled backstage. Catching a glimpse of Samantha, I briefly smirked. Well, at least she's going to lose all the money she'd put in the Gwen and Tim dating poll. I hope she'd bet a lot, too.

"Dinger!"

To make matters worse, Brittany was glaring down at me *again*. "You can't sit there while there's work to be done." She huffed. "Go clean up the paintbrushes."

Ugh! I was not even able to lick my wounds before Brittany found work for me to do.

I grumbled to myself while I squeezed and rubbed all the paintbrushes clean, alternately imagining each as a different face. It must've been preoccupying therapy, because I didn't even really notice when a girl came up behind me.

"Um, excuse me." She was impatiently tapping her foot against the floor, reminding me too much of Trixie.

"Do you need a brush?" I asked innocently, just to irritate her.

Apparently, I was not the only one who had annoyed her today. "I was sent to get another one," the girl explained in a scathing tone. "Raiya needs it for adding orange to the background."

"Okay, why orange?" I suddenly asked. "There's no orange on the balcony."

The girl sighed like I was stupid. (I guess I was surrounded by particularly moronic and temperamental people today.) "It's for the sky, not the balcony, duh."

"But the sky's supposed to be blue." Even I knew that, and I didn't particularly care.

The girl shrugged her shoulders. "Raiya didn't want it to be blue, I guess," she answered, a bitter tone in her voice. "She's too good for *that*." The girl nodded toward the upstage area, where another girl in a khaki Rosemont uniform was crouching down in front of a familiar-looking case.

So it was *her* case. I almost laughed as I half wondered if she really could carry it around. She was definitely scrawny. And her hair was a mess, too.

I handed a brush to the impatient girl in front of me before she sulked back to the stage without another word.

"Dinger!" I saw Poncey waving me over. "Where have you been, Dinger? I could use your help lugging the stuff up from the music room. It's heavy!"

"You're a football player. You're supposed to be strong."

"I know, but it's a lot of junk. Plus, I'm still hurting from dragging all those bags in earlier."

"You sure complain a lot, Poncey," I said. "That's not the kind of attitude that's going to get you a scholarship—or a girlfriend."

"Yeah, yeah," Poncey muttered. "Let's see how long it takes you to get irritated."

146

C. S. JOHNSON

I found out, to my dismay, that Poncey was right. A large supply of chairs, bandstands, and music sheets still needed to be moved, in addition to the instruments. I groaned and cursed appropriately.

After my sixth trip, I came back down to find Poncey breathing heavily as he tried to move the harp. It was the last thing to go, but I guess Poncey was too weak to move it on his own. "Ah, is the poor little Ponce tired?" I chuckled.

"No, is dumb-head Dinger still trying to raise his English grade using alliteration?" Poncey shot back.

"Wow, it's not every day I hear you use big words," I replied. "Okay, I'll help with the harp."

"Just get it yourself."

"If you're tired, why don't we take a break?" I suggested. "Betcha the harp won't be needed for another ten minutes anyway."

"Yeah, good idea." Poncey flopped down on the stool behind the harp. He laughed and put his hands on the strings. "Hey, Dinger. Do I resemble an angel?"

"Angels don't exist, Ponce," I replied. "People just say they do so they feel better about stuff."

I relished getting to tell him the bad news. It was fun to tell the children Santa Claus didn't exist.

Poncey shook his head. "You're so narrow-minded, Dinger."

"What?!"

"Yeah. You can't prove they don't exist, and people have seen them and everything. But you can't believe in them, so you just block the entire idea out. That's called being narrow-minded."

"No, that's called being logical."

"Ha! Logic doesn't always happen with the miraculous." Poncey smirked. "Take that." He laughed as I stared at him, a disgusted/dumbstruck look on my face. "Anyway, don't you think I look good like this? I'd make a good harp player, I think." He strummed a few of the strings, making a jargon of noise that sounded not *too* bad but still completely horrible, considering Poncey didn't know how to play.

I grinned. "Let me try," I insisted. "I'll bet I can make it play better."

Poncey laughed again and moved so I could sit in the harpist's seat. "Go ahead and try," he taunted me.

I reveled in the challenge, dramatically stretching out my fingers. "Just watch," I said, arranging my hands on the harp like I'd seen on TV.

That's when it happened again.

My mind swept away as I was suddenly tangled in my alternate reality. "Huh?" I was back in outer space like the times before, in the hospital, in class. And this time I was fully engaged, and fully aware I had a right to be petrified.

Wildly, I tried to shake myself out of it, like it was some

THE STARLIGHT CHRONICLES

spastic condition in my brain that I could control. "What's going on? I don't like doing this anymore!" I shouted. "I didn't ask for this!"

A soft laugh whispered behind me.

My back went icy with prickled awareness. "Huh?" I knew that laugh. My heart simultaneously stilled and beat faster.

I felt a hand on my arm. The voice tickled my ear. "Close your eyes."

"What? Why?" I asked. "Who are you?"

"Please, trust me," the urging gentleness whispered. "I'll show you."

I uneasily closed my eyes. (Against my better judgment.) Instantly, a pair of small hands intertwined with mine, and guided me as I plucked and strummed the harp, perfectly in tune.

Now I couldn't resist; I opened my eyes, and turned around.

"Huh?" I blinked. I was back in the classroom, playing the harp harmoniously, with Poncey staring at me, his mouth agape. I would've laughed if I wasn't so preoccupied with my own wonder.

"Wow! How do you do that?" Poncey asked, amazed.

My hands fell off the strings, shaking. "Was I playing the entire time?" I asked.

149

"What? What do you mean? You just sat down and started playing like a pro," Poncey told me. "And hey, it was really good, too. Really, really good. I'll bet if you composed a song on the harp for Gwen, she'd forget Tim and come running to you."

All of the wonder and amazement dropped out of me as reality brutally slapped my face.

"Sorry … " Poncey muttered, seeing my stricken face. "I heard some of the other guys talking about what happened with Gwen and Tim and everything."

It was time to work, not to brood, not to think, not to care. I shook off my sadness quickly enough. "Well, let's get this harp moved, anyway."

Just as we finished hauling the harp up to the auditorium, Gwen beckoned us. "Hey, guys," she called out. "That run was pretty good, don't you think?"

"If you mean my running back and forth for the music equipment, I disagree," Poncey quipped. "Sorry, Gwen. We didn't catch your performance. I'm sure you broke a leg, though."

More like a heart, I grimaced, recalling how she and Tim are oh-so-magically in love now.

"No!"

I'm jolted out of my bout of self-pity as a familiar voice raked into the far reaches of the auditorium, following a loud clanking noise. Almost instantaneously, everyone grew silent.

It's apparently time for a *real* show.

The noise, I saw, came from Courtney throwing down her paintbrushes. It was disturbing that I could see, as far back as I was, anger clearly etched onto her no-longer-pretty face.

I was more surprised Mikey wasn't the one on the receiving end of her tantrum. It was that girl. Raina ... Raiya? Whatever her name was.

"Wonder what Raiya did this time?" Nearby, a group of Rosemont girls were muffling their giggles as they whispered excitedly.

"I think it's brave of Raiya to stand up to Courtney," another girl said.

"Shush! Do *you* want to go against Courtney Knox? She was the most popular girl at Rosemont. Besides, Raiya's just getting in Courtney's way."

"I suppose you're right. Poor Raiya."

I sighed. Girl talk was so shallow and pathetic. Talking about the social pyramid when I was nearby was almost insulting to me.

There was a smaller banging noise and a loud "Oof!" all of a sudden. I looked over to see that Courtney had just tried to storm off, but she accidentally sunk her foot in a paint tray and tripped over it.

I had a hard time not laughing, so I gave up and snickered loudly. Others joined in quickly and with little persuasion. Courtney turned a flaming red, making us all laugh harder.

"Augh!"

"What's that all about?" Gwen asked. I commended her for her question; things are often funnier with the whole story.

Gwen was answered by one of the giggling Rosemont girls. "Well, apparently, Courtney was upset at Raiya for painting the backdrop."

"Oh, that's all?" Gwen shrugged. "It seems like a lot for something so little, I'd say."

Mikey and I both watched as Courtney came stomping down the aisle toward us. Her face had a sour look on it, like a dried-up raisin. It did her no credit to have her nose stuck up in the air like that, either, her face scrunched like a half-melted Barbie doll.

I smirked at Mikey. "Still going to ask her out?"

Mikey didn't take his eyes off of her retreating form until she was gone. Then he shook his head. "Nope."

"Twenty dollars."

"Nope. Couldn't pay me to."

I snickered. "I'll say this—detention might be bad, but it's definitely entertaining."

Gwen sighed wearily. "I wish this wasn't happening. Tomorrow is opening night, and the last thing we need is conflict … "

I stopped listening to her soon enough. It wasn't that I

didn't respect Gwen, but why didn't she bother Tim? After all, she was *Tim's* girl now, right? It was not my job to make her feel better.

Gwen finally caught on to my non-attention. "Hey! You aren't listening to me, are you?"

Apparently she was irritated by that. "You know, Gwen, you're really being too selfish about it," I said, before calmly walking away.

I heard Mikey and Ponce laughing even harder than they had at Courtney's departure, and I felt good, despite leaving at odds with Gwen.

Well, she *was* being selfish. She was too busy being caught up in her own problems to see that I had my own life.

I walked up onto the stage, just to look around. The balcony piece was dry now; Courtney's mediocre painting was permanent. Imagining Tim trying to climb up and having it break amused me. That would be *hilarious*!

Out of the corner of my eye, I saw Samantha walking in my direction. I scampered aside, deciding it was best to duck out of the way.

"Oof." I found myself cursing softly but no less urgently as I tripped. "What the—?" I looked down to see a night sky. The backdrop.

A small sun near the bottom captured my eye; it was painted a darkish-red color, with surrounding yellow and orange clouds that faded into pink, and from there became purple, which then turned into a dark blue. Huh. The orange *had* been a good call. "Wow. That's really good," I whispered.

It was almost real enough to dream under.

A small movement flashed in the corner of my eye. I turned, but saw no one there. "Huh … " I could've sworn I saw something.

I didn't have time to worry about it. The detention bell rang, and I was free. *Free at last!*

☼11☼
Attack

The rain seemed to match my mood as I walked toward the school once more; a full week of nonstop rain had passed. But I couldn't be sure whether it was the rain, or the mess with Gwen and Tim that made me raw and awful.

Rawful, I supposed.

"It's not my fault," I muttered to myself, splashing through the puddles. "How could I anticipate Gwen would feel sorry enough that drama geek that she would say she had 'feelings' for him? Those feelings could easily be pity, as much as love."

I just hadn't had the best week, I told myself. First we lost at Homecoming, then I got detention, then I was stuck at play practice for detention, and then the girl I'd deemed lucky enough to go out with me decided to hook up with Rodgers and Hammerstein's long-lost great grandson.

I sighed, looking up at the sky, a small part of my mind worried that it was worse than that, too. There was also the question of my sanity, the condition of my brain, or the conspiracy of my company to consider—the flashes of alternate realities haunting me since the meteorite struck.

The images, which I once thought were peaceful and welcoming, like a private island for the mind to wander off to occasionally, had begun burning and stinging into my very bones—although that might've had something to do with the fact I kept falling asleep in drama class.

Earlier that morning, I'd woken up from a dream of some

155

sort, with my back and arms stinging and my head pinching with pain. My eyes had been blurry, but I could've sworn my arm was glowing at first, too.

It wasn't even that weird of a dream, except for a couple of things.

There was this woman in it. Her skinned was some kind of blue color. I called her Maia, the name I'd assigned to her from the other dream I'd had.

She seemed familiar to me as she lounged about. She'd taken a nap in the sky, high above all the city rain. I saw her as she dozed peacefully, while something like a servant or a minion punched out rain, thunder, and lightning on the city below.

I looked up at the sky as I walked onward to school, and in between blinks, I shook my head. There would be no way to see if that were even remotely true. Clouds usually ... I faltered. Looking up again, I saw just rain falling. "There are no clouds."

"There are no clouds." Then it was another dream that scourged my mind. The girl. That's what she'd said as she looked up at the sky.

"That's weird," I murmured slowly. "Huh." I shook it off as best as I could. The power plant one town over must've been experimenting with nuclear power again. I pushed the thought aside as I relentlessly marched on through the rain.

One day I would run out of excuses. One day this relentless pursuit would end, and I would be flooded with new

156

revelation. The shadow of light that haunted me would one day be the death of me, and I would no longer be able to shade the truth to my liking.

But it was not yet that day, thank goodness.

I welcomed the sight of Rachel's Café like a lighthouse on the shore. Perhaps Jason was inside. I was hungry, and it was a good place to look for a distraction.

"Hey, Jason's friend," Rachel called out as I walked through the door. "How are you?"

"Hi, Rachel." I waved back. "I'm okay, I guess."

Rachel smiled. "You're lying, I can tell."

"How?" The word escaped me before I could stop it. Slipping up because of the weather, no doubt.

"No one's having a good week. I don't expect any different from the expression you had as you walked in here."

"I guess you're right. It's been a bad week. I would like some decent food to help it out." It hadn't helped when I arrived home from the worst day ever the day before and right away noticed two critical things: Estella-Louise had left a bowl of Vegan-O's cereal (ce-"unreal") and organic almond milk for dinner ("Boy, someone's getting lazy," I muttered), and the refrigerator had nothing in it like meat or anything looking relatively normal. Or anything I could recognize.

Rachel got up from her stool and put on fresh coffee. "I'll make you a chai blend," she offered. "It'll cheer you up."

"Thanks."

As Rachel handed me her special chai latte and a plate of cookies, the news popped up on the TV behind the bar. I barely paid attention—only enough to know I was truly and undeniably bored.

"Good evening, it's been a wet week in Apollo City," Jack Anchorman started out with a clearly forced grin on his middle-aged, made-up face.

"Yes, that's right, Jack," Patricia Anchorwoman keyed in. "But there is more concern elsewhere. In medical news, hospital officials are still stunned as they have yet to diagnose the cause of the latest sickness going around town. A serious outbreak last Friday night at the Falcons-Tiger game at Apollo Central High sent twenty-seven people to the hospital. While there have been reports alluding to foreign or domestic bioterrorism, individuals are highly cautioned to be on the lookout for signs of sickness or mysterious activity."

I stilled, almost frightened. Friday's game. Bioterrorism? Sickness?

"Awful, isn't it?" Rachel asked. "It's so weird how that all started up."

"How many times must I tell you, Rachel?" an angry old voice piped up. Rachel's kooky grandpa was sitting nearby. I inwardly groaned.

Grandpa Odd leaned forward. "It's not a sickness," he declared. "It's got to be something else."

"Like what?" I asked, despite myself.

"It's a curse, no doubt about it."

Voodoo was not something I believed in. I (wisely) turned my attention back to my food. "You make the best stuff," I told Rachel, glad to change the subject. "What kind of cookie is this?"

"Chocolate strawberry-banana." she smiled. "It's organic, too."

"Oh, I didn't know that," I muttered disdainfully. "My mother's on a crazed vegan diet this month. She's trying to lose weight I think, even though she's already thin enough."

Rachel laughed. "Sounds like the average woman, that's for sure. Although I'd never go vegan for that." She pulled out another cookie and bit into it. "Seriously, if I was fat, I'd make fun of skinny people."

I broke out in snickers. "That's great! I like your food. At home, Cheryl's got a chef who comes in and makes her stuff, but it's always like grass-clipping casserole or baked soybeans. You should be her cook."

"Oh, that's a nice offer, but this is my home." Rachel grinned. "Literally. I live right on top of the bar with my mother and cousin ... and Grandpa, too, though he's supposed to be in a nursing home right now."

"I told you I'd never go back," Grandpa Odd spoke up. "I don't need anyone's help to survive."

Rachel rolled her eyes. "Yeah, sure, Grandpa. Since you're

159

so capable, why don't you go and hang up that new picture? I just got it from the framer's today."

"Are you kidding? That's a job for a young whipper-snapper. Why don't you ask him to do it?" The old man huffed into his cup, nodding at me. "When will the young learn common sense? The tragedy of youth … "

"Eh, what?" I didn't understand him. The words were easy enough, but the meaning?

The eyes of the old man twinkled from beneath his old ragged hat. "The tragedy of youth … lamentable!"

"Grandpa, enough. He's becoming one of our most valuable customers," Rachel scolded him.

As Rachel and her grandfather started arguing, I smiled down into my near-empty cup. It'd been a good visit. It's always nice to be reminded that no matter how much life sucks, someone else has it worse.

And I was glad for the reminder, as I was about to make my life even worse.

I'd been coerced into seeing the play.

The thunderstorm the night before had managed to keep a lot of students up much later than usual—most of them go to bed at two in the morning anyway—but it was the play's opening night. That was reason for some kind of celebration, to some anyway, meager and unimpressive though it was.

Gwen was especially bubbly, I noticed as I watched her from behind the stage, a sour look no doubt hanging on my face. It's probably because she gets to make-out on stage with Tim. Gross.

I want it known that I only went to the play for three reasons.

One: My parents had insisted on it. And they are paying, and I am duty-bound to take freebies from my parents whenever I can.

Two: My teachers all offered extra credit for seeing *Romeo and Juliet*. Yes, our school district was that poor. They had to bribe us to overcome our apathy.

Three: My friends had made extensively detailed plans to mess up the play with catcalls, water balloons, and funny noises whenever possible. As you can probably guess, that was the reason that *really* won me over.

I amused myself all day with images of Tim going in to kiss Gwen and having a water balloon lunged at his face instead. For variety, I altered what I'd put inside the balloon. (Everything from pudding to paint slipped through my imagination.) I'd had to stop myself from snickering at my visual imagery more than once.

And people say kids don't have any imagination anymore.

THE STARLIGHT CHRONICLES

I smirked as Lockard, dressed in puffy Italian robes, gave his little opening spiel.

"Welcome! Blah-blah-blah, blah-blah, Frank Lockard, blah-blah, *Romeo and Juliet* ... blah-blah, blah! And now, for our play!" (I didn't even hear half of it.)

"Hey, anyone want a water balloon?" Poncey asked as Drew made obnoxious snoring noises.

"Hey, guys," Simon said. "Tell me when it's at a death scene, so I can laugh hysterically."

"Hey, quit elbowing me!" Jason muttered. "And save the balloons for later; the dying scenes aren't serious until the end!"

"Come on, I was thinking we'd throw one right at the prologue guy to ruin it right at the start."

"Why did I come again? And why did I decide to sit with you guys?" I asked, slumping down in my seat. Subtlety was beyond them, obviously.

"Hey, shut up," Mikey replied. "I don't care what you guys do, but make sure it's at the right moment. Timing is everything here."

The prologue guy, Garrett Kafka, dressed up in Italian robes similar to Lockard's, came out from behind the curtain. I had to laugh. Kafka was a popular senior, but we had never gotten along very well; we never really traveled in the same circles, I guess. But I knew him enough to know his ego was taking quite a hit for not being the star tonight. I imagined the silly costume did nothing for him, either.

Holding a scroll, Kafka began to read monotonously, "Two households, both alike in dignity, in fair Verona, where we lay our scene, from ancient grudge break to new mutiny, where civil blood makes civil hands unclean. From forth the fatal loins of these two foes, a pair of star-crossed—" He choked as a water balloon hit him square in the stomach.

My friends and I, along with most of the audience, howled with laughter. (Just to be fair, there were *some* people who gasped in horror at Garrett's misfortune.)

A light flickered, and then Garrett—along with my gut—stilled. The auditorium went dark. Kafka's uneven, raspy breathing could suddenly be heard over the microphone on his shirt. And all I heard was the sound of him hitting the floor. Fainted? Dead?

I couldn't tell from where I was sitting. But it wouldn't be the first time a performance at Central killed someone.

"What's going on?" Drew asked. "No one's supposed to die this early. And I didn't get to do anything yet."

"Neither did I." Poncey looked around. "Could this be part of the direction?"

Suddenly the emergency lights flickered on. The transfixed blank stare on Kafka's face I could just make out in the poor emergency lighting reminded me all too much of what happened at the Homecoming game.

Full of dread, I made my decision. "I'll be back," I said,

jumping up from my seat.

The key was finding that guy I'd seen before—the limping man in black. He was the culprit again, surely. That was my plan, and I was sticking to it.

Then thunder exploded. A bolt of lightning crashed through the ceiling and stuck the stage; it splintered and dusty figures flew up as it cracked underneath Kafka's body. We all unanimously cringed as Kafka's body thumped onto the desks below.

"Ah-ha!" I boasted, largely to myself, as the stage splintered and a gaping hole suddenly appeared. I'd been right about the stage workmanship.

Time for a new plan, though.

Out of the upheaval of dust and debris, a human-like form appeared in a blast of smoke and sparks; it was a woman, I could just make out, with messy, curly hair, and a blue-colored skin tone ... *Uh-oh.*

It took me only a split second to recognize her from my nightmares. Which I guess weren't really nightmares anymore.

It was Maia. My brain started screaming. *It's Maia!*

"Ladies and gentlemen, there has been a call for new casting. Allow me to provide some enticing new entertainment." She, with her smurf-colored arms, pulled a man out of his seat. "I need your assistance in my magic act," she crooned.

"Wait! Stop! What are you doing?!" Mr. Lockard came out running, almost tripping over the hem of his long, ridiculous outfit. "This is not your play."

I wished at this point I'd been less shocked. I would've enjoyed Lockard's humiliation much more if I hadn't been frantically wondering what was wrong with me.

Maia grinned at him. "Oh, I see. You'd like to go first!" After hastily discarding her captor, she grabbed Lockard by the neck and hoisted him up. One frightening moment later, frazzles of light came pouring out of Mr. Lockard's mouth. He screamed, and then slumped over seconds later.

The light from within him curled up and settled into the palm of Maia's free hand. She tossed his limp body on the floor. "Yes, this is what I wanted."

Most of the audience was looking from Mr. Lockard to Maia with expressions of horror, like they'd just seen a cat get run over by a car. They were waiting for Mr. Lockard to get up, but after a long moment, when he still hadn't moved, everyone started screaming.

"Help, get us out of here!"

"Did you see what she did to that ugly man?"

"She killed him!"

"I want my money back!"

The big crowd made its way to the nearest doors, but it was no good. Even I could see from where I was that all the doors were locked and sealed shut. Probably with a supernatural lock, too.

We were all pathetically trapped and helpless—and with some kind of soul-cannibal on the loose. I could not contain my laughter as I tried not to freak out.

Who says dreams don't come true? Mine certainly were coming to life tonight. Literally.

Maia began eagerly picking up more audience members to drain. I randomly thought how I'd never seen such gusto. I laughed again. *Everything is going horribly wrong,* I thought as my eyes prickled with tears of madness.

"Dinger, what's your problem?!" Mikey screamed at me.

What was wrong with me, indeed? Was I simply dreaming again, going mad, unable to tell waking from sleeping? Or was I truly faced with a reality that was so unreal I'd yet to process it?

I heard Gwen screaming and something inside me snapped. I wasn't crazy. Well, maybe I was. But Gwen was *real,* and I knew I had to protect her once more.

While everyone was screaming and scrambling, I bustled up onto the stage to make sure Gwen was safe. The rain drippled down from the gaping hole in the roof onto my face, blurring over my vision, stalling my rescue, and hiding my hidden inner turmoil.

"Huh?" I suddenly stopped short, seconds before everyone else.

A bright beam of white, hot light shot out from a dark

166

corner of the auditorium.

In the brief second I saw it, I swore it was an arrow. "An arrow of light?" I wondered. Weird.

Well, why not? We'd already gotten a blue fairy-turned-vampire type of warrior sucking the life out of the audience.

The streak of light struck Maia at her feet. She jumped back and fell, right into the drama classroom below. (I decided I would properly laugh at that later.) Her power was momentarily broken. The doors suddenly burst open, and everyone hurriedly rushed out, stampede style.

I was grabbed by an overwhelming wonder; I *had* to know whether or not this was being televised. Or recorded.

A familiar scream brought me back to the problem at hand.

"Gwen!" I called out, resuming my search for her. Where was she?

"I'm over here!" Gwen called out. She grabbed my arm as she nearly ran me over. "What's happened, Ham? What did that lady do to Mr. Lockard and Garrett and those other people?"

"I don't know what," I told her honestly. "But they're not waking up, so I assume she killed them."

"What?!" Tim gasped as he suddenly came up beside us.

"Yeah, we have to get out of here, now!" I yelled. I was so glad not many were people backstage. That made running to the exit much easier.

Gwen abruptly turned around. "I forgot!" she called. "Tim, go on without me! I have to get Raiya!"

Tim looked at her uneasily. "All right, I'll make sure everyone else gets to a safe place," he called out before resuming his run.

"What?" I looked at her incredulously. "No, just go, Gwen!"

"She's in the student lounge near the band room! She was sick earlier. We have to get her out of here, too!"

"I'm sure she's already gone," I shouted, pushing Gwen through the exit. "Besides, I think this lady wants fresh victims, not sick ones. Go!"

"We have to—"

"We're leaving!" I finally took her by the shoulders and directed her out the door. She relented a moment later, but she wasn't happy about it. At least she'd be alive to hate me later.

Outside, people scrambled to get away from Maia, while some, freshly drained, flattened themselves out on the street, the relentless rain sprinkling all over them. I watched as Maia licked her lips. "The souls of humans sure are tasty." She smiled evilly as she turned to face us.

Great. We were the only ones who were twenty yards or less away from her. There were others running down the street already, but Maia let them go.

Up close, I had the full effect of Maia in real life. In my

dreams, nothing was completely clear, nothing certain. There was a façade, a veil, which separated me from the true darkness of her essence.

But now the rainy night sky darkened with her appearance, poisoned by her radiation. Everything with even the smallest amount of light and life in it was chased away.

The pale ivory of her gown contrasted sharply with the glowing of her eyes. And while she'd mostly been eating souls, she hadn't stopped herself from sucking up some blood, too. It was all over her hands and face as she fixed her gaze on Gwen.

"Such a pretty girl," she murmured to Gwen, who heard her and trembled.

"Hammy … we have to escape … " Gwen whispered to me.

"I know, that's what I've been telling you. Let me think of a plan."

"Hurry," Gwen pleaded with me. "I think I'm going to throw up."

Maia continued walking toward us. "You must be Juliet. Well, well … we all know what happens to Juliet in the end, don't we? Too bad about your performance tonight, but we both know I'm a better star."

Without thinking, I jumped in front of Gwen. "If you want her, you have to go through me, you … you ugly smurf-hag!"

"Fine with me, insolent boy!" Maia cried out, striking me in

169

the head; I wasn't quick enough to dodge it.

I went reeling as Maia laughed cruelly. "I'll get to you in a moment. I want to claim my proper title of 'star of the evening' first!"

That's when a light flashed and the rain stopped. The thunder clashed out once more before it went silent. A moment later, another ugly creature fell to the ground.

"What's this? Gibliom?" Maia asked, hollering at the monster freshly fallen from the sky. "What's going on? Get back up there and make it rain again!"

I did a quick double take. What was she talking about? She was the reason for the horrible rain this week? It figured. Then I recalled the vision of her relaxing on her cloud while this monster—now that I see him—ran around brewing up the thunderstorm. This was her minion!

"My Lady." The monster struggled to get off the wet ground. "There's something—"

Another flash of light. He was knocked onto the ground, flat on his face. Gibliom still moved, but he was trembling.

I couldn't take my eyes off this thing; he was just so ugly. His skin was dark blue-gray, with wrinkles on his wrinkles and wispy, snake-like hair and eyes that burned scarlet.

It was then that I heard it. The lulling tune of a harp poured out from nowhere. My familiar melody. I stilled. It was the song from my dreams.

Maia heard it, too, and seethed. "I know that melody … "

170

she whispered. "Show yourself!" she commanded.

The tune became louder as I looked all around. "There!" I cried out as I saw her.

There was a girl, if she could be called a girl, on the roof of the school building behind us. She was standing tall, playing the harp next to her. Her long brownish-red hair gave her an element of grace, even as the rigidity of her armor lent her strength.

Gwen saw her and gasped. "She's lovely."

I felt like saying the same. The girl was no ordinary girl. She had wings—white wings, like an angel. A smaller pair of wings fluttered out of her head, while a pair of glimmering silver chains draped over her forehead were pulled into the half-bun at the back of her head. A long, bright-red feather dangled in her hair, contrasting pointedly with the blue and violet of her leather tunic.

She finished the last line of her pretty piece and then snapped her eyes open.

I felt a twinge inside me. Even from this far away, I knew her eyes were a captivating shade of violet, speckled with starlight.

"Who are you?" I couldn't resist the urge to ask.

She didn't answer me, but turned her full attention to Maia. She held up a half-gloved hand and reached into the sky. A second later, a bright arrow appeared in her hand, and her harp transformed itself into a bow.

171

Maia took a step back.

Gwen was whimpering, and this was perhaps the only thing that made me realize it was a good time to try to escape. It would be easy to use the distraction to get us out of there …

"Maia, you have done well up to this point," a new voice called out from the sky. "Why do I have to come to your rescue now?"

I didn't have to look up to know who it was now. Everyone and his brother had shown up. Why not Orpheus too?

"Orpheus!" Maia cried out. Her fro-like hair whipped around as she turned her attention to the newcomer.

Hovering in the sky just above the school was a dirty-looking man wearing a black cloak-like outfit. The long robes mostly disguised a wrinkly, repulsive body, but didn't do anything to contain the smell. The rotten-eggs aftershave wasn't going to get him a girlfriend any more than the comic-con outfit.

"Yes. Yes, it's me," Orpheus replied, confirming my suspicions. "What seems to be the problem?"

"It's—"

"A what? A block in your brain?" he asked as he floated over to her.

I smirked, briefly forgetting the imperative nature of the situation. He might smell bad, look horrible and not be a nice guy, but I liked his insults.

"No—look!"

Everyone looked back toward the angelic warrior. I didn't blame Orpheus for getting angry a second later.

"What?" Maia gasped. "She's gone?! I swear, Orpheus, there was a person standing up there a moment ago!"

"You're not supposed to be afraid of people—you're supposed to attack them." Orpheus sighed.

I suppose people will wonder why Gwen and I didn't just run away. You have to understand that this was not something you get to see every day. After years of reality TV shows, you should know by now the power a dysfunctional family has over its audience.

So it was only when Orpheus looked down at us that we snapped back to normal fear mode.

"Let's just hurry up and get these two, and be done for now. You know we need their Soulfire."

Soulfire? Okay, so reality TV had just turned into science fiction. Or maybe fantasy?

"Psst! Dinger!" I looked over and saw Mikey beckoning me from behind some brick columns. I almost rolled my eyes; Mikey wasn't seriously stupid enough to think a brick wall could fend off these evil magician-electrician people, was he?

But better to be behind a wall than out in the open. I grabbed Gwen by the wrist and pulled her along behind me as I ran for cover.

I flinched as Orpheus suddenly appeared directly in front of me. "Augh!" I screeched to a halt, falling over; Gwen followed in suit.

"Hammy!" Gwen cried out as she landed hard on her right side. There was a snapping noise, and horror sneaked into me as I saw Gwen's hand bent back on her arm. I felt sick.

And Orpheus wasted no time.

He grabbed me by the wrist. A strong stinging sensation flew up my arm, my teeth clenched in severe, excruciating pain, and I struggled not to scream (loudly). I trembled as Orpheus laughed. It was the same cold laugh I remembered from my dreams.

Why do my dreams only come true when it means certain death? No, it's never for true love or winning the championship title.

I went back to being concerned for my life as another sizzle of power crept through my body, setting my nerve endings on fire. "Stop it!"

"You've been enough trouble!" Orpheus cried out, laughing. "I'll burn your body and suck out your soul, and then we'll see how much trouble you cause!"

Orpheus and I were too caught up in his moment of glory and my moment of life-altering agony to see the arrow. It sliced through the air and dug into his left eye, squirting what looked like a stream of runny black acid all over his front. The force of impact and injury rattled him enough to let me go.

"Augh! Ouch!" Orpheus cursed loudly. He clenched his teeth as he jerked the arrow out a moment later; the eye popped out along with it, nearly making me vomit on the spot. And while the flood of pain stopped drowning my body, I was still physically reeling from the forceful shadow of his power.

"You see? I told you!" Maia called out. "She just moved!"

Orpheus looked over with his remaining eye to see the warrior with the violet eyes staring down at him. I followed his gaze as I fell to my knees, trying to recover.

She narrowed her gaze. "Let him go!" she called out. Her voice was strong. I was just about to ask her for her name when she added, "Your battle is with me, not these children."

Children?! *Children?!* Anger blistered through me as I squirmed, trying to get out of the ugly weirdo's grip. My earlier pain was nothing compared to the rage fueling me now!

It took Orpheus only seconds to agree. He discarded me simply and easily enough, straight into the window of the school.

The shards of the glass shattered underneath my weight as I rolled through. When I opened my eyes (and peeled my hands from my face), I found myself sprawled out on the floor of a classroom.

I struggled to sit up and catch my breath. I crawled over to the window sill, trying to pick the glass fragments out of my bloody hands. The wrist Orpheus had gripped scourged with pain.

But there was nothing to be done about it. There were other things needing my attention. As I managed to get a good look out the window, I saw Mikey peek his head out from behind the wall, gawking at the archer-girl.

Gwen was curled up on the ground less than three yards away from Mikey, obviously scared to death.

Orpheus stared up at the angel/archer. "Who are you?" Orpheus asked. "Where did you get that bow and arrow?"

"Why don't you tell me who you are first?" the fighter responded, a charming sneer on her face. "Who do you serve?"

Orpheus grinned. I guess he liked her, at least enough to humor her, which made me angry for some reason. "Very well. I am Orpheus, the future ruler of this planet. I serve my Master, the Ruler of the Void."

I watch the bow tighten as the eyes narrowed, as if to deny that. "We shall see."

Gibliom, meanwhile, was steadily gaining back his strength. I saw him breathing deeply, and I knew he would make his move soon. There wasn't much time to make a plan.

Orpheus continued his speech, "I will be the one to turn this world into one of complete emptiness. I will rule over it, at the right hand of my Master."

"Gwen! Look out!" I called. Gibliom was fully back to his old self, conjuring up a ball of lightning in his hands.

"Augh!" Gwen screamed frantically. She struggled to get up off the ground.

The bow tightened hard, and the arrow of light was released. It shot forward, cutting through the side of Orpheus' arm and digging its way into Gibliom's chest; the creature hollered as his essence began to fade away.

"You shall return to the hellish realm from where you came," the archer-girl told him firmly. "You belong back in the memory of this world, and the void of your own, but nowhere else."

Before I could breathe a sigh of relief, Orpheus lashed out an attack of his own against her. The black flames licked at the air where she'd just been standing. "I don't know who you are, but you will die for what you have done!" he cursed, as his arm and eye socket continued to bleed out his oozy blood.

It's now or never, I decided. I made my move while they were fighting.

I hopped over and scraped Gwen off the ground. "Run!" I told her, tucking her good arm over my shoulder.

"Dinger!" Mikey hurried over from his hiding spot and carefully took Gwen's other arm and wrapped his arm around her waist.

"Come on," I said. "Let's head towards the park. It's big and there are plenty of places to hide."

"What about her?" Gwen asked, nodding to the pretty

soldier as she dodged another attack while unleashing one of her own.

"She can take care of herself, obviously." I snorted indignantly. I was still not happy about her "children" remark from before. "Let's worry about us."

By the time we reached the entrance to Shoreside Park, there were a couple of ambulances and fire trucks heading toward the school. Some police cars were even pulling over closer to where we were; no doubt they were trying to get some information from some of the others fleeing the scene.

"Now they come!" I exclaimed in exasperation. "Honestly, it's been a horrible week for timing."

Mikey and Gwen ignored me as they babbled together. "Mikey, did you see that girl?"

"Did I ever! She's amazing!"

"And she's so graceful! How kind of her to save us from those monsters."

"Did you see her shoot? Perfect aim and release. She got those guys bad."

"Did you see her hair? I'll bet that she goes to the most expensive hair salons in town."

"I'm going to ask her out on a date next time I see her."

"Uh, guys? Hello?" I waved my arms persistently to get their attention. "People trying to kill us, remember? We've got to move."

"But they're not following us anymore." Gwen protested.

"Yeah, Dinger. Are you blind?" Mikey frowned. "We're talking about something way more important here, anyway."

"She saved our lives, Hammy! We owe it to her to be her friend and thank her," Gwen insisted.

"I'm sure that's exactly why you want to find her, too." I rolled my eyes, annoyed. If I saw her again, I was going to make it clear to her *I* was no more a child than she was.

☼12☼
Starry-Eyed

Mikey, Gwen, and I slowed our pace upon reaching the park. It was close to the school, but there were a lot of ideal hiding places to veg for a while, which we needed for more than one reason.

Gwen yelped as I examined her arm. "Hey, watch it." She pouted.

Geez, I never knew Gwen could be such a wimp, I thought. After all, Gwen used to be a cheerleader. They didn't take whiners on the squad, only winners—or so the catchphrase went. She'd quit for some reason unknown to myself; I'd just assumed it was because she was trying to focus on getting her grades up. Her parents were pushy when it came to that, I knew.

"You think she broke it?" Mikey asked.

"Looks like it," I said. "I should know; my dad's a doctor."

"Yeah, a *heart* doctor."

"Shut up. I still know the basics. It's not like my dad became a doctor overnight," I retorted. I looked back at Gwen's wrist. It was swelling, and there was a definite limp to its appearance. "You'll have to go to the hospital," I said. "You'll need x-rays."

She sighed. "Will I still be able to play Juliet?"

I nearly choked. "Are you kidding me?" I asked. "You were almost killed, and your concern is for the play, which is the

180

whole reason you were there in the first place? Wow, that's touching and sad at the same time." I roll my eyes when I am sure she is not looking.

"I know," Mikey agreed. "But, Gwen, think of it this way— who else knows all your lines that can perform your role? And, even if there are others, who would willingly take the title away from you?"

"You're right." Gwen sighed and slumped over, relieved but still slightly depressed.

"Besides, the play is probably going to be canceled now anyway," I told her. "So you shouldn't have to worry about it at all."

Gwen glared at me. "They *won't* cancel it. You know, you're so rude sometimes!"

"Well, Mr. Lockard is dead or something, so you don't have a director. And anyway, if I really were such a rude person, this wouldn't be the second time I've saved your life," I reminded her abruptly.

She softened, but I could tell she was still reluctant about it. "Sorry," she mumbled. "Thank you for saving me again."

"You're welcome." Despite the forced tone, my ego swelled with pride.

"You know, that girl saved you, too." Gwen smiled. "I guess that makes me indebted to her even more."

And then my ego popped, just like a balloon. (What was it with Gwen and crushing my pride lately? I had to wonder.)

181

"We don't owe her anything," I declared. "Gwen, think about it like this, if she wanted to really save us, she would've done it earlier, when all the people were running free and stuff. She was just waiting around for the best moment to get what she wanted."

"Well, what was it that she wanted?" Mikey asked. "Because once I know, nothing will stop me from getting it for her. She's the most beautiful woman I've ever seen before. I must know who she is."

Gwen and I exchanged wry looks. "Whatever." We shrugged. It was just another girl in the phase of Mikey's affections. It usually happened every week. Or every other day. Nothing special about this one.

"I'm serious you guys!" Mikey insisted.

"Good, good, that's nice," I agreed.

Gwen sighed. "You guys are awful!"

"Then allow me to take them off your hands," a new voice offered.

"You wouldn't want them—" Mikey's sentence died fast as he looked up. I turned to see a pair of dark eyes gleaming under the skin of a policewoman. "Uh, can I help you ma'am?"

At the sight of the blue face, I backed up immediately. "Guys, it's her," I hissed. It was the smurf-lady in disguise! "Let's get out of here."

"What are you talking about, Hammy?" Gwen asked. "It's

182

just a cop."

"No it's not! It's her! Are you blind?" I shook my head. No time to worry about the ability of my best friends to properly discern what was happening at the moment. "Excuse us, ma'am, we're just heading … to the docks," I lied. "We're in a hurry."

"Not so fast!"

Mikey tried to back away, but it was too late. The "cop" grabbed for him just as he tripped, falling down.

I picked up Gwen. "We've got to move!"

We were hit by a blast of dark power as we tried to turn away. Thrown through the air once more, before I (less than gracefully) crashed into a tree, while Gwen skidded across the grass.

Mikey started hyperventilating, scurrying away from the deadly woman as fast as he could manage. He backed up into a large boulder and fainted.

"Humans are amusing, that's for sure." Maia laughed.

The ache in my back grew as I stumbled to get up. Weakness had overtaken me. There were scratches from the broken window, and a large bump on my leg from the pavement. There's nothing I can do, I realized.

I collapsed in the shadow of the tree, torn between fighting for consciousness and letting myself exit this living nightmare. Fighting won out, mostly because I was sure I would just have nightmares about this later, whether I was awake or not.

"Hammy!" Gwen cried out to me. "Hammy, no!"

The demonic eyes of the blue lady glowed scarlet. It was all over now.

Maia grinned, her nails sinking into Gwen's shoulders. "Girls have so much life," she told Gwen. "Let me take some of yours off your hands. It'll make things so much easier. You won't have to do anything at all; not anything. Wouldn't it be nice to rest?"

Gwen had an entranced look on her face. Her fear had paralyzed her beyond emotion. Or something like that, something where she didn't have to care about anything, and something where she was unbelievably tired. "What are you talking about?" Gwen asked.

"I'm telling you you're overworked. You need rest, a long rest, to heal, to gain strength and energy … wouldn't you like that?"

"I have been working hard," Gwen admitted softly.

Don't give up! I wanted to shake her. *Don't give into this creepy lady creature.* I was helpless to stop her. "Gwen, don't do it," I whispered, even though I knew she couldn't hear me now.

"I'm here to help you … to help you find rest … " Maia said to her. The nails sank in harder, a black steam rising as she released toxins of deceit into Gwen's blood.

"Stop! Let her go." I groaned to myself.

Whoosh.

"What?!" Maia flung around just in time to dodge the arrow of light. It whizzed by her, missing her by only a breath.

Gwen smiled lazily with recognition and hope. "She's back."

I looked over to see the sight. I was not disappointed. Even in the night time, the warrior maiden glimmered with a bright aura.

Maia rolled her eyes, her own angry aura flaring. "Just who do you think you are, anyway? This is no time for games, little girl!"

The "little girl" squared her shoulders, ready for battle. "I am Starry Knight," she called out. "And I will not let you harm these humans anymore! Their Soulfire is their own, and not for you."

"Oh, boy," Maia muttered. "This isn't good."

"The Bow of Righteousness never fails to stop evil," Starry Knight called out, warning Maia. "I sent Gibliom back to the darker realm where he belongs. His demon spirit is gone, cast away."

"Will that be my fate as well?" Maia asked sarcastically.

There was no answer. Just a hardened glare.

I was confused; terribly, terribly confused. What in the world was this girl talking about? And why was she saying things more appropriately found in a video game?

Was I insane? Was this even real?

"Very well." Maia sighed. A ball of blue energy formed between her hands. "You must die!"

If the battle had *not* been as fearsome and awful to behold as fights usually were in the movies, I might have noticed the small shadow creeping toward me.

I could hear him, somewhat, but I was more distracted by the action going on in front of me; it was like ignoring the person in the movie theater who insists on talking on his cell phone during the show.

"This is it? What a pitiful excuse. Not much to work with. I would've preferred the fighter-girl over there to this boy lying here."

There was a sigh. "This better not be some kind of joke," the gruffness muttered. "I'm going to tell if it is. Wake up!"

My eyes drowsily winked over in the direction of the voice. "I am awake," I slurred. My arm and back tingled like they'd fallen asleep, and I was starting to feel burning hot. "Who're you?"

"Who am I? I'm your only hope of surviving at this point!" the voice answered. "Now, get up. You've got to help Starry Knight. You've got to seal away the Sinister."

186

"What?" I squinted into the distance, looking around the park. Where's the voice coming from? And what is it talking about?

There was a sigh. "I'm down here, kid!"

I looked down and nearly fainted. The oddest creature I'd ever seen was looking up at me. It looked like a kind of lizard-snake or mutated eel. "Where are you? I don't see anything but this ugly reptile," I said.

The "ugly reptile" rolled its eyes. "Uh, I was the one who was calling you, kid. Are you some kind of idiot? After all these years living here on Earth, I guess you've finally lost your mind."

"Hey! I'm not an idiot!" I replied. "I have the highest grades in my class, you thing, you!"

"The name is Elysian." The lizard-snake huffed indignantly. "And where we're from, grades don't matter, remember?"

When I just stared at him, mouth agape, he sighed and continued on. "All right, are you awake enough to fight?"

"I'm not awake at all," I remarked. "I'm sitting here, talking to an iguana like it's a real person … " my voice trailed off. "This has to be some kind of dream. But it's nothing at all like the other ones I've had."

Elysian put his claws on his head in exasperation. "Oh, no. This is never going to work!"

There was a loud explosion. Gwen screamed as one of Maia's power attacks came dangerously close to hitting

Mikey.

"You see? You're not dreaming!" Elysian yelled at me. "You've got to help."

"How can I help?" I asked, anxious and fearful and probably about to vomit. "I can't fight these things! They're not even human. At least, I don't think so—"

It was Elysian's turn to just stare up at me. "You mean you don't remember?" he asked incredulously. He clawed his way up my shirt and stared me in the eye. "You really don't remember?!" Elysian shouted. "That's impossible!"

"How do you know what's impossible? I'm stuck in the middle of a park in the middle of the evening talking to some strange gecko thing while watching the wrestling channel for some alien network! Is that impossible to you?"

Elysian chuckled for a moment, obviously forgetting the task at hand in light of the question. "Yes, *that's* impossible."

"Augh!" I turned to see Gwen getting hit by a blast of energy. She slumped over, motionless.

Resolve found its way into me at last. I stood up, grabbing onto the tree I'd been flung into for support. "My friends," I murmured. It was time to stop playing with my imagination.

I didn't have the strength to fight. But I had to. I had no choice. I less than eagerly started to head over. I was only a few yards away from Maia when she turned on me.

She smirked. "Still alive? Try this!" She threw an energy ball straight at me.

Regret conjured itself in me as quickly as she'd conjured up the attack. My life started to flash before my eyes as the space between me and pain exponentially disappeared. The only coherent thought in my mind was that there was no way to escape ...

"No!" My eyes, squeezed shut in preparation for pain, suddenly opened for a quick peek. I gasped.

Starry Knight had jumped in front of me, shielding me from the attack.

It hit her square on. She tumbled into me, and we were forced backward. Before I could think, I wrapped my arms around her.

All of a sudden, I was screaming. Not with pain, but with something else, something more than pain. Uncontrollable suffering. I barely noticed that Starry Knight also had a pained expression on her face as she was forced away from me by the torrential winds of the attack.

As I looked over at her, my blood started pulsating. My forehead was blanketed with sweat. The pain in my back left, but there was this feeling like something was there ...

My hollowed heart racing, my mind lost in confusion and outrage at this injustice, my very soul seeming to cry out. I screamed again as a powerful beam of some kind of white light burst out of me, lighting up the night sky.

Maia screamed, cowering in fear. She hurried away as my energy shot up, engulfing the park in a sea of light. One flicker of blue light against the blackness of night, and she

189

was gone.

Elysian looked on thoughtfully as I slumped over, exhausted and breathless, but no longer feeling as though I was on fire. "Maybe this will work after all," he murmured.

The power flow ceased. I stood up, straighter than before. My wounds were gone, and I felt normal again.

I saw Starry Knight stirring from her position on the ground. *That's right, she'd just saved me. Again, I guess.* I thought about maybe saying thank you, when she briskly picked up her bow and started walking away.

"Wait!" I called after her. She stilled for a moment, but kept walking. A second later, she leapt into the air. Her wings caught her, and she was soaring off into the night.

Elysian came up to me as Starry Knight's retreating figure slowly faded away. "You did well," he praised. "Not bad at all for your first try."

I flinched. "You're *real*?!"

Elysian sighed, flicking his scaly tail. "You just frightened away one of the most deadly forces to all creation, and you're concerned about me?" he asked. "That's rather illogical, even in human terms."

"Well, who are you? What are you?" I asked skeptically.

"Me? Well, my name is Elysian. I am a Celestial Dragon. A changeling."

I felt like laughing. "A changeling dragon?"

190

Elysian huffed. "I am able to appear in other forms beside a dragon, can't you see? Do your eyes work right?"

I should've known then and there Elysian was going to be a pain. I am amazed to this day that I didn't catch on sooner to his annoying self.

"Yes, but I've never seen one of those before." *And don't want to for a long time*, I reminded myself silently.

The dragon-lizard was very odd. It was a lot smaller than the traditional dragon, for one thing—if it weren't for the wings, it would've looked like a regular, though severely beat up, lizard of some sort. His body was long, covered in scales, with dark green, bat-like wings on the back, and smaller ones on his feet. His eyes were green, a glowing yellow-green, and they held a mix of hardness, pity, and impatience.

"Well, it's a rare race of dragons, indeed." Elysian straightened with proud dignity. "Even in the Immortal Realm, there are not many." He folded back his wings, so they disappeared into his scaly back. "Now that I'm here, you just tell your family I'm your new pet."

"Whoa, what makes you think you're coming home with me?"

"Shouldn't you be checking on your friends?" he asked. "It's getting rather late, I'd say."

I frowned, but the ugly dragon, or whatever it was, had a point. Gwen still needed to go to the hospital for her wrist and whatever else was broken thanks to Maia and her attack.

191

☼13☼
Marked

I sigh as my mother either berated or commended me over the phone; I wasn't really certain what she was saying, because Adam was with her, tearing his room to pieces, and my cell phone signal was low inside the hospital. *Just smile and nod*, I thought.

That's the best way to handle parents like mine. Just smile and nod.

Gwen was getting fixed up in the emergency room while Mikey was looking for some food. I'd been wandering around in the waiting room when Cheryl called. She'd apparently walked into the house with Adam, turned on the news, and almost had a heart attack. At least that was how it sounded.

"Yeah. Okay, Cheryl," I interrupted her. I'd lost track of the conversation enough.

"That's no way to address your mother, Ham!"

"Got to go," I said as I hung up.

There was a smirk on the tiny face of the dragon. "Family issues?" Elysian asked.

"Why did you follow us here, again?" I glanced around nervously; I didn't want anyone to see me talking to what looked like a deformed snake. "I don't think they let animals in here," I informed Elysian.

Elysian puffed. "You need me."

"No, I don't. I was fine—better than fine—before you came along."

Elysian cocked an eyebrow. "Oh, really? You'd rather live in ignorance your whole life than know what is really going on?"

I gritted my teeth. "I can see what is going on just fine."

"Ah, so you know how you got that mark on your wrist, then." Elysian's smirk grew. "And you know all about the power you emitted a while ago, I see." He smiled mockingly.

"What?" I looked down and saw there was indeed a small, black four-pointed star on the underside of my wrist. The image of that dream, with that girl, flashed through my mind's eye. She'd been looking at a mark on her wrist. Was it possible … Was she Starry Knight?

"How did that—how did you—did you do this?!"

The tiny dragon glowed, transforming into the shape of a chameleon, before hopping up on my shoulder. His eyes glistened arrogantly. "You see? You *do* have questions."

"How am I going to explain this to my parents?" I asked, staring at the unwelcome mark in disbelief. "They're not even letting me drive until I'm eighteen. I can't tell them I got a tattoo. Tell me how to get rid of it!"

Elysian looked away. He was silent for a moment, and he seemed to be rather fidgety.

"Oh, great. You don't know either." I snorted. "Thanks a bunch."

"Well, I don't know." Elysian huffed indignantly. "But you won't get close to figuring it out on your own. Just calm down."

"Calm down?! Are you crazy?"

There was a tap on my shoulder, and I jumped about a foot in the air. Mikey stood behind me, trying hard not to laugh.

"Hey, man," he said. "Who're you talking to?"

"Uh … Cheryl called, apparently in hysterics." Blaming the parents nearly always works.

"You fighting with your parents again?"

"You mean my ex-parents," I corrected him. "I'm suing for divorce the moment I turn eighteen."

"I don't recommend it." Mikey smiled. "You know Cheryl. She could whip you and get the legal right to do it."

Mikey had a point, I silently conceded. "I guess so. I still need them for college money. Maybe I'll wait until I'm twenty-one."

Mikey laughed and held out the extra cup he had in his hand. "Here's some coffee for you."

I smiled as I sipped. *Ah … there's nothing in the world like the rush of bitter beans ground up with extra caffeine.* "Thanks. Did you see Mark anywhere?"

"No. This is the emergency room, not the heart floor," Mikey reminded me. "We can't be sure he'll come anyway, you know. He might be in surgery."

"Yeah, I suppose," I agreed. "Gwen still hasn't come out."

"I sure hope she's okay."

The concern etched on Mikey's face confused me slightly before I recalled Mikey was the one who'd introduced me to Gwen back in junior high. I'd suspected Mikey even had a crush on her for a while, but they were just good friends now.

Still, I supposed Mikey was entitled to feel a bit more worried than what the situation usually required. It's not often someone gets injured by a *real* monster.

"I'm sure she'll be fine," I told him, trying to shift his attention away from me. Elysian was still clinging to my sleeve in a very casual, almost unnoticeable way. I hoped the stupid dragon was smart enough not to get himself noticed while we were in the company of normal people.

Mikey slouched further down into the uncomfortable chair. "You know, people are going to start thinking our school is cursed or something." He laughed, almost nervously.

"Yeah."

"I mean, Rosemont was destroyed, but there were fewer injuries there than there were at Homecoming, and now the play." He looked over at me and asked, "Do you think it's possible some kids from Rosemont were in on this? That the rivalry between our schools has finally led them off into the deep end?"

I shrugged. "I don't know. But if they did, that smurf-lady
196

and monster-guy have some pretty realistic costumes."

"Yeah, you're right. I bet it was just a bunch of kids. After all, Rosemont was a private school. Over half those kids are rich."

"Who do you think that girl was? The one with the bow and arrows? Was she in on it, too?"

Mikey grinned. "Even if she was, I know who she is."

"Really?" I looked skeptical. "Who was she, then?"

"She's my next girlfriend."

I groaned. "What makes you think she's real? Maybe we just had a hallucination."

"More than one person can't have the same hallucination, Dinger. That's just stupid."

"Well, what about age? She could be older than you."

Mikey contemplated this. "Well, there's no way of being sure, but even if she turns out older than me by five or six years, I could adjust to it. Now, younger would be more of a problem, but I could wait."

I was about to ask how he intended to find her again, when Gwen came out with her parents. "Gwen!"

"Hey, guys," Gwen greeted us with a tired voice.

Jody, Mrs. Kessler, ran up to me and threw me into a hug. "You saved my baby!" she cried. "Again!"

197

Mr. Kessler was more sedate. He reached out his hand to me. "Thank you, son. We're indebted to you for protecting our Gwennie."

"No problem, Mr. Kessler." I smiled as I shook his hand.

"Call me John," he said warmly.

Gwen was blushing, probably from her parent's embarrassing display. But I was hoping it was for other reasons, too.

"Are you feeling better?" I asked her.

Gwen's eyes glittered with happiness. "Yes, thanks to you and Starry Knight I am." She smiled. Indicating her arm, she added, "It's only a broken wrist, but the doctor told us I was lucky, compared to the others from Central." She looked at me curiously for a moment. "What about you, Hammy? Where are your bruises?"

"Uh, what do you mean?" I asked, vaguely recalling how I had been miraculously healed.

"You were thrown on the ground and through a window. Not to mention into a tree. I thought you had some cuts earlier."

"Well ... " I (briefly) glared at Elysian, who smirked up at me with an "I-told-you-so" look on his face. Another riddle to solve. "I must've just looked like I was scraped up. I have no idea what you're talking about. Hey, is that my dad over there?"

Here's a good hint. Awkward conversations are easily

remedied by changing the subject. And it's best to change the subject to something connected to the conversation or environment. That way you won't be called on it.

Elysian snickered into my sleeve.

"I don't see him," Gwen said, craning her neck to see down the hall behind her.

"Gwen, honey, we'd better go," her mother called out to her. "It's late."

"Coming! Give me one moment," she called back. Gwen turned her attention back to me. "My mom told me school was canceled tomorrow."

"Well, I guess I'll see you on Monday then." I squeezed her good shoulder affectionately.

She pushed through my shoulder pat to give me a hug. "Yeah … thanks again, Hammy. I really appreciate you saving my life." She looked over at Mikey. "I owe thanks to you too, Mike, for helping to get me out of there."

"It's nothing. It's what friends are for." Mikey smiled brightly. "Who else is going to help you out when you're being chased down by a monster from outer space?"

Conjuring up a mental image of Starry Knight, I wisely said nothing. (For once.)

☼

199

"Eek! A snake!"

I shuddered at my mother's shriek. It was late, and everyone was usually in bed. But thanks to the monsters, I'd lost eight dollars for the play, gone to the hospital, and worst of all, I found myself suddenly sharing my room with an annoying dragon—a dragon which my mother had no doubt just found sneaking around the house.

"Cheryl, you can be *so* annoying," I muttered to myself as I made my way downstairs.

I found my mother having her conniption as she stood on the armchair in the living room.

"Uh, what's wrong now?"

Cheryl pointed to the couch. "There's a snake under there! I saw it! I saw it!"

"It's not a snake. It's ... well ... I kinda forgot to mention, I brought home a new pet today."

"What?"

"Well, it's like a project. For biology. It's not a snake, either; it's um ... " I scratched my head. "Changeling dragon" wasn't really a common pet for anyone. "Well, he's a rare lizard Mr. Elm wanted me to take care of for a while ... since I'm doing a report on it." Yeah, that's it. Brilliant. Another brilliant imaginary fabrication.

"You're sure it's not a snake?"

"Positive," I promised.

"Well, good." She exclaimed as she climbed down from the chair. "Next time you do something like this for school, ask Mr. Elm for a permission slip for me to sign!"

"Won't happen again, Cheryl."

She frowned. "I'm your mother."

"Good to know," I muttered, heading for the stairs again. I'd learned over the course of my teenage years that, the less I dealt with my parents, the more I seemed to like them. But I could tell that wouldn't be a good long-term remedy.

"Ham! Pick up your lizard before you go, please. And make sure he stays in your room. I wouldn't want Adam frightened first thing in the morning. His nanny will be coming over tomorrow, and we don't need another reason for her to hesitate."

"Why is she coming here tomorrow?" I scrunched up my face at the thought of Mrs. Weatherby, Adam's nanny. She was a pill. Who needed to take a lot of pills.

After a moment of careful thinking, Cheryl pursed her lips and said, "After the attack at the high school tonight, I thought it best for you and your brother to stay here with someone tomorrow. It would be safer."

"What?" I knew school was canceled, but I was not just going to willingly stay here. I had several more attractive offers to either make or consider—Jason's, Mikey's, maybe even Gwen's house.

It was the wrong thing to say to Cheryl. She barked back at me. "Hamilton! Do you know how many people were taken to the hospital? Do you know how many are being quarantined tonight? Your father will be stuck at work for the whole weekend, and the police have nothing on the attackers. Nothing! It's too dangerous. Now get your lizard and get to bed." And with that, she left me alone in the living room.

Years later, I would be astounded at myself for not being more worried about the crew of monsters and their potential to harm people. I supposed it was largely due to Cheryl's uber-concern for the situation. My mother was completely backwards in her thinking, and I disagreed with her on practically everything as a teenager.

I walked over to the couch. "Elysian, what were you thinking?" I mumbled.

The glowing dark eyes narrowed. "If you hadn't kicked me out of your room, I wouldn't have been seen."

"My room is upstairs," I shot back.

"You kicked me out!"

"Shut up already."

There was a slight noise behind us; I looked over to see Adam with an unusual expression on his young face.

"Er … hi there, Adam." I waved.

"Hammonton." Adam smiled shyly. He took a cautious step closer, hugging his organic-cotton stuffed panda bear.

I backed away. "Good night!" I called, turning around and breaking into a run.

Safe in my room, dragon clutched in my fist, I exhaled. Whew. That was close. Adam didn't say a lot, but it only took one incident to make a mess of an already-confusing situation.

Elysian transformed back into his smaller form as he jumped up on the bed. "I didn't know you had a brother."

"Yeah, he's only three. Doesn't talk too much. Cheryl and Mark think he's autistic or shy or something."

Elysian huffed. "There's nothing wrong with him. He's just intuitive."

"What do you mean by that?" I asked, putting my skeptical face back on.

"Children sense things older people don't. I think he knows I'm not just some 'rare lizard.'"

"Hey, I couldn't think of anything else to call you," I replied defensively. I was suddenly very tired. Tired and tired of. This whole mess tonight had me upset, confused and half-crazy. I still wasn't done processing it all. "I hope you don't snore," was all I said to the lizard before slumping over.

"A mansion this size is big enough for both of us," Elysian grumbled as he curled up on the edge of the bed.

It was so hard, even as this small animal-thing was drifting off to sleep in front of me, to believe this dragon was for real. For *really* real.

I looked up at the ceiling as thoughts about Gwen and the events of the evening swirled around me. Haunting me. Taunting me. Terrorizing me.

While there had to be a reasonable explanation for it all, there were none that came to me. And without an explanation, it was just better to ignore it. That usually worked.

But I was getting tired of running from all of these things. And I feared the day when I would be devoured alive by the truth I refused to acknowledge.

It was this fear that ripped through me as I drifted off, hoping to dream. But for all my exhaustion, I couldn't find the peace of sleep.

I scrunched up my face, trying to block it all out.

The girl who saved me tonight jumped into my head. Starry Knight.

She ... well, I didn't like her, I knew, but there was something about her I just didn't get. "Elysian?" I asked, sitting up. "Elysian, who was that girl with the bow and arrow and wings and stuff?"

When the tiny dragon just snarled sleepily, I rolled my eyes in exasperation. But I let the picture of her settle into my mind. I decided I'd much rather think of her than the fear swiping at me.

☼

The dream started out as normal, but it wasn't far in when I could tell it was going to be a bad one again.

The light unveiled the haze to reveal their faces, and I knew it was too late to go back to the nothingness. A moment passed, and then I heard their voices. It was almost like I was one of them, but they couldn't see me.

"Maia, Maia, Maia." Orpheus sighed, his half-mutilated face coming into clearer focus. "You managed to get some supply of power, but it is hardly adequate; not to mention you consumed most of it yourself."

She shrugged. "I would've gotten more, if it hadn't been for that Starry Knight person, or whoever she was, and that strange kid." I knew she was talking about me.

"I see. You're going to blame your failure on human children?"

Maia's eyes snapped up, unusually alert for someone as lazy-looking as her. "I'd hardly call their powers human." She huffed. I had to agree with her. But I didn't want to think of what it made me if I was *not* human.

Orpheus sighed again. I got the feeling he did that a lot with Maia. "I don't believe it. Starry Knight is one thing, but to blame your shortcomings on a high school teenager and his friends … that's a new level of low for even you, Maia."

"Yeah," the one I'd named Elektra agreed. I faltered here in my vision, as I took a good look at her. Her orange glow left

205

me thinking about cheap tanning lotion.

"Maia, you're so lazy," Meropae, the pinkish-toned one, complained. "There are plenty of people out there to coax into giving us their souls. You think you were just so unfortunate as to find the only four who would resist? And on top of that, you managed to get our beloved ally, Gibliom, thrown from this realm?"

"I almost had the girl," Maia shot back. "If it hadn't been for that Starry Knight person, I would've succeeded."

"Sure, sure," Alcyonë spoke up. I didn't know if I'd ever seen her before up close. She looked sick; her skin was greenish in color. Made me think of the Wicked Witch from *The Wizard of Oz*. "You're just jealous the rest of us have more power."

Orpheus cleared his throat. "Excuse me, ladies, but let's not forget, Maia did bring back more than anyone else this week, small and relatively useless as it is. I say she goes out again. As you all well know, slothfulness is one of the easiest deadly forces used to access humans. And it is one of the most readily available, too."

Slothfulness? What the heck is that? I was not sure, but I thought it meant laziness. Yes, that's it. And I supposed that would explain why Maia was so lazy, if her chief power source was laziness.

The others huffed, rolled their eyes, or just stared with no particular expression at all.

Orpheus' one eye blazed at their reaction. "This is not a

game, you incompetent morons! Do you think it is funny, that you will run out of energy and be forced into the Prince's submission? Might I remind you, we are trapped here until we can gain enough power to break through Time?!"

"Orpheus, just—"

"No! You girls need to take this more seriously. You have no idea how fortunate we are to be here on Earth."

What is he talking about? I wondered.

"If we'd been properly sentenced, we would have been sent back to our prison—or even worse, sent to the broken realm where our master resides! Do any of you want that?"

"No." Several of the sinister ladies muttered that out quickly enough.

"Fine. I want to see more effort." Orpheus nodded. "Maia! You have until the end of the week to redeem yourself."

"Oh, all right. I'm going then." She slouched and dragged her feet along the floor as she walked out of the darkened room. The scenery, even though it was darker than night, looked familiar. It had to be somewhere in the city.

"Great," Maia spit out bitterly, "another mission where I have to work. This is getting ridiculous."

And then I woke up, sweating and breathing heavily, in my bedroom, but feeling more than a little out of my mind.

THE STARLIGHT CHRONICLES

☼14☼
Sidetracked

I walked down the crowded school hallways, waving to my friends, who catcalled me from all angles, and said hello to some teachers, surprising them with sincerity. (I knew they would more likely respect me if I faked respect for them.)

School resumed on the Monday following the attack, along with some sense of normalcy, for which I was grateful. You have to admit, as much as school was a bother, it had its perks. A few, anyway.

The damage to the school was reported, despite witness accounts to the contrary, as due to thunder and lightning. The play was postponed until further notice. The football game against Shoreside was rescheduled for the following week. I couldn't really complain, but I would if asked for my opinion on the matter.

After all, I had a reputation to consider.

My school was small, especially for a public high school—probably because it was in the older part of town. I'd lived in the Lake County Heights, a subdivision basically created for the most financially secure families of Apollo City, for nearly all my life now. Cheryl and Mark had moved to the city when Cheryl was first promoted in her law firm. And Mark, well, he was a cardiologist; he could find work anywhere as long as there was a hospital around.

But Apollo Central, in my opinion, was a good school for me. Here, I was the popular guy nearly everyone liked, and everyone else was too jealous to like. I liked that better than going to some prep school where mommies and daddies were the only reasons students could brag. I was better than that. I was cultured and mature. I was capable of making other people envy me on my own.

I usually enjoyed going to school, though I was smart enough not to admit it. But there were a few days when I considered school a hassle or problematic.

Such as when Elysian followed me to school.

The small dragon had ignored me for most of the weekend, primarily because I intentionally avoided him; I'd been "busy" calling Gwen to see how she was doing, going over to Mikey's house and Jason's house, sleeping in late, and other important things like that—trying to forget all the things I'd seen and heard and felt.

It wasn't easy, but I managed to succeed. The dreams that haunted me were crushed by a relentless onslaught of scheduled activities.

I sighed, watching Elysian through the window as he transformed from his lizard-shape to a snake. This week was already starting to look bad, I thought gloomily. It had been predicted to be so, and it was the final week of the football season, on top of everything else.

Mrs. Smithe smiled as the bell rang. I thought she looked a lot more cheerful this week—although that could have been said of a lot of people, since the apparently cursed rain was gone and the sun was out again. "Okay, class, time for your exam. I hope you all studied hard over the weekend." Everyone gave her a blank stare until we all, simultaneously, recalled it was the day of our huge test.

No wonder she was so happy.

"Crap!" Drew punched his fist down on his desk. "I completely forgot. I'm going to fail."

"Me, too," Poncey added. "I thought for sure Martha would push it back until Tuesday, at least."

I personally felt stricken. *Of course* today was the exam worth fifteen percent of the final grade. *Of course.* I put my Game Pac away and sighed.

It had been years since I felt unprepared for a test. But the test was passed out before I could even try to pass out.

"Okay, class. Do your best. You have both periods to finish."

I, along with the rest of the class, groaned and grumbled in response.

"Psst! Hammy!"

I looked to see Gwen waving in my direction with her arm in a newly-covered cast. "Good luck," she whispered.

I winked at her. "No problem." I waited until she turned her attention back on her test to shudder at the thought of mine. Shooting one last angry look at the tiny dragon nonchalantly slithering his way up the waterspout, I sighed and began filling out my answer sheet.

An hour and a half later, I walked up, handed my test to

Martha, and left the room, not saying anything. Worst test ever, I decided as I left feeling more than slightly empty inside.

I was about to walk out of the school Gwen came up beside me. "Did you do all right on the test today, Hammy?"

"Hi, Gwen." Warm surprise trickled through me at her presence. It wasn't every day that I managed to get some time in with Gwen before heading home. "Test was a piece of cake," I lied brightly and brilliantly. "Martha's going to have to try harder to stump me next time."

Gwen laughed. "I didn't study at all," she admitted. "I forgot about it entirely. I hope I don't fail."

"I'm sure you did fine," I assured her. "You can study with me next time."

Gwen nodded. "I might have to. You always do so well on her tests."

"Well, your house is on my way home. If you'd like, I can stop by today and we can compare notes."

As I said it, there was an uncertainty in Gwen's expression that made me feel uncomfortable. She was still smiling, and I was still hoping she would make this easy for me and just say yes. The next few seconds felt like eternity as I waited for her answer. She was about to respond when—

"Hey, Gwen. How are you feeling today?" Tim suddenly popped up beside her. It was more than a little creepy. Like stalker creepy.

"Oh, hi, Tim." Gwen smiled. I was a little surprised to see her hesitate when she saw him, too. "My arm's doing as well as expected."

Tim slowed down a bit. "Are you headed to the meeting?"

Gwen and I both stopped and turned our attention to him at last, no doubt making him even more nervous. "What meeting?" Gwen asked.

"Ms. Carmichael's here from Rosemont, in the auditorium."

Gwen frowned. "I don't remember any play practice being scheduled."

"I thought maybe Ms. Carmichael would have information about the play reopening," Tim muttered, glancing around nervously. He caught my eyes long enough for me to know he was looking for a convenient exit.

I relaxed a bit; Tim had been tamed. He was no longer any threat to me. Of course, I would never admit to him having been a threat in the first place …

Ha! Looks like he finally figured out his proper place.

"Is that all right with you, Hammy?" Gwen asked, looking directly at me. Her question brought me back to the situation at hand, only to see Tim and Gwen both waiting on an answer from me.

"Huh?"

Gwen patiently repeated what I assumed was the same question she'd asked me while I hadn't been paying attention. "I asked you if you would like to come to the meeting, and then we could head home."

"Oh. Oh, sure," I readily agreed. I didn't relish the prospect of going to anything drama-related, but getting to walk Gwen to her house was suitable compensation. "Sounds fine to me. Let's go." I nodded to Tim, who took the hint, and began to lead the way to the auditorium.

We arrived just in time. "I'm so glad all of you were able to make it here today," Ms. Carmichael announced as we walked in. "I am so sorry it's because of such horrifying circumstances … "

I found out a bit later Ms. Carmichael was the art director at Rosemont before the terrible events with the meteorite. She'd willingly volunteered to help Mr. Lockard finish the play at Central while her unemployment/disaster relief paychecks were delivered.

I glanced over to see how Gwen was taking all the news about the play. I frowned when I saw her cringe. "You okay?" I asked. "She's not upsetting you, is she?"

"Yeah. My arm's still hurting a bit," she whispered back. I nodded in understanding; according to the doctor, Gwen's fracture was not severe, but Gwen had mentioned it more than a few times she wished it would stop hurting so much. Obviously, the pain medication had worn off after the long school day.

" ... I just wanted you to know Mr. Lockard will not be returning. The, uh, incident at the opening night performance has apparently sent his system into shock. He is in the hospital, in the special care ward."

At Ms. Carmichael's conclusion, there was little remorse expressed for Lockard; I don't think they hated him, but it was clear the students were more upset that he wouldn't be around to direct the play, than at what had happened to him.

Gwen raised her hand. "Ms. Carmichael, why can't you direct the play this week so we can reopen?"

A small smile made its way onto my mouth; Gwen had a lot of innocence and hope and everything that made me feel like it was possible there was still some good in the world. It was part of the reason I liked her. And to be honest and fair, it wasn't impossible for the play to reopen; after all, the auditorium was fixed up (just needed cleaning now), and the stage was mostly repaired. But I knew, even before the response came, that the answer was going to be no.

"I'm sorry, Gwen," Ms. Carmichael apologized. "I already went to the school board, asking in light of Mr. Lockard's condition, if I could step in. I'm afraid the reparatory arts have been placed on hold until next year."

"That's stupid," another student spoke up. "We've been working so hard, and they're going to throw it all away because they're afraid of having to pay money?"

Ms. Carmichael sighed. "It's very complicated. Even if Mr. Lockard was well enough, there is little chance that the play would go on."

She continued on, assuring them she wanted to be able to work with them again. There was other stuff, like how the students should make sure everything was in order, and … the list went on. (There's always a list teachers tell the students and the students don't think it's necessary so they don't listen and usually end up regretting it later.) I didn't even bother to listen to it; I just watched as Gwen listened, and I knew how to respond just from looking at her reactions. Her face faded from hope to disappointment to resigned acceptance as Ms. Carmichael took questions and eventually dismissed everyone.

Gwen looked out into the audience seats and dropped her head, miserably.

"I hope you don't feel too sad," Tim told her, putting his hand on her shoulder gently.

"There's nothing you can do," Gwen told him. "I'll see you later, okay?"

Gwen and I watched as he left, downcast at Gwen's dismissal more than the news. Gwen then turned to me. "I'm going to walk around for a few more moments, okay, Hammy? Then we can head to my house."

"Sure," I agreed. "Take your time." I hesitated briefly before adding, "Do you want me to walk with you?"

"No, I'll only be a moment or two. Be right back." Gwen

smiled her best "I'm okay" smile and then walked backstage, behind the balcony set.

I waited until she was out of sight before I whipped out my phone, using it as a decoy as I mentally did a small victory jig. *Yes! Gwen and I are going to hang out at her house! Tim's out of the way! Everything is going my way at last! Hey, that's almost a rhyme. I wonder if I could get it to rhyme? Eh, what would be the point? It's not like I could sing it in front of Gwen anyway. She'd kill me for being that callous.*

I put my phone down and looked up to see if Gwen was coming yet.

Instantly, I frowned. Gwen was talking to someone on the stage. I couldn't tell who it was, and that was reason enough to worry I would have to deal with another contender for Gwen's affections. Anger began to boil within me as I saw the shadowed figure reach out and put a hand on Gwen's arm.

Before I could decide to head on over to "interrupt," the figure let go of Gwen, and headed off the stage.

Gwen smiled as she looked up at me. "I'll be right there," she called out as she started in my direction.

"Great." I waved back, more than glad to see her coming back to me with some of her renewed cheerfulness.

My happiness was short-lived, of course. The happiness inside of me popped like a soap bubble at the voice from behind me.

"Yes, it's great. I'm dying to get out of here."

I groaned instantly. The voice was coming from my backpack, and it was the last one I wanted to hear. That *thing* was getting annoying. Really annoying. "Elysian, I thought I told you to stay home!"

"Well, I told you plenty of things, too, and you don't listen to me at all," the tiny dragon huffed as his dragon faced poked through the opening of my backpack zipper.

There are moments when all the world comes together, and everything is right. And then there are moments like that moment, when you have a dragon in your backpack and you know he is not going to let you enjoy hanging out with the girl of your dreams.

I sighed. *There goes my afternoon with Gwen.*

"You can't follow me to school!" I nearly shouted on my way home. The newly November air was chilly, but I didn't realize it as I glowered at the tiny dragon on my shoulder. "What do I tell people if they see you?"

"You can't keep ignoring me, or your mission." Elysian huffed angrily.

"I'm not ignoring you. I'm *yelling* at you! And I don't know what mission you're talking about." I seethed.

THE STARLIGHT CHRONICLES

Elysian shook his head. "I was under the impression you were mourning this weekend, so I let you be. But now I see you were just trying to ignore the truth, so you could get on with your life."

"So?" My voice nearly cracked. A couple of people passing by me on the street gave me funny looks. I glared at them and waited until they were out of sight. Then I turned back to Elysian.

"Now, where was—" I started to hassle Elysian again, only to see he was gone from my shoulder. "Huh?" I looked around, feeling my anxiety build. I could only imagine what someone would say if they saw a dragon sauntering down the street. "Where'd you go?"

I caught sight of that slimy tail of his soon enough; Elysian had disappeared to look into a window across the street.

I hurriedly picked up the small animal, nearly choking it as I tucked it halfway inside my backpack. "What are you doing?" I asked through gritted teeth. "You're making me mad."

Elysian snarled. "I'm making *you* mad? Excuse me, but who's the one in charge here?"

"What do you mean?" I narrowed my eyes. "I'm in charge of you, not the other way around!" And I shook my backpack with Elysian inside to prove I was the bigger, stronger one.

"Uh, Hamilton?"

Oh, great. Someone had seen me.

I looked up to see Rachel smiling down at me from an

open window. "What are you doing?" she asked.

"Uh, nothing. Hey, Rachel."

She gave me an odd expression before waving me in. "Come on in, I've got a new drink I want you to try."

"Okay. Be there in a minute." The second she left, I glared at Elysian. "What were you thinking, coming over here? You're in the human world, where no one has ever seen one of you before. You'd be placed in a museum, or a zoo, or maybe a freak-show carnival faster than you could say—"

"Are you coming?" Rachel asked, opening the door.

"Uh, yeah. Just making sure all my stuff's here." I lied.

"Oh … well, come on in. Business is slow right now. And Grandpa Odd's here, just warning you."

Ah, no wonder she was bribing me to come inside. Grandpa was home.

"Judgment Day's coming!" The old man greeted me with a raised drink.

Rachel rolled her eyes. "He was reading O'Connor earlier, if you're wondering. She is one of his favorites," she explained as she handed me a drink. "This is a pumpkin chai smoothie. It's sugar-free, low-fat, and full of healthy nutrients."

"And yet, it tastes like a regular, drinkable pumpkin chai smoothie." I smile after the first sip. I had an over-appreciation for the normal things in life lately.

"Judgment's Day's coming," Grandpa Odd squeaked up again.

"Uh ... Rachel?" I raised my eyebrows in a silent question.

"No, he's just insane. I don't let him drink."

Grandpa Odd was slouched over in his chair, his head down on his folded arms, almost like a student in a boring class. I tried not to laugh. "He's well named, really. I've never met anyone so 'odd' before."

Rachel grinned. "That's part of our family's Norwegian side. We're actually related to the founder of Apollo City, Ogden Skarmastad."

I supposed that explained the insanity. It was hereditary.

"Judgment Day's coming!" Grandpa Odd straightened.

"You'll see! When Judgment Day comes, no one will be expecting it."

"But if you know it's coming, then doesn't that mean it's not coming?" I snorted.

The old man looked at me intently. "Just because I know it's coming, doesn't mean it won't. It's coming soon, but you will not be expecting it ... not expecting it at all." He leaned in closer and added, "And you won't escape the consequences—or having to making a choice ... " Then he sat back down and began to brood into his cup once more.

Elysian was mesmerized by Grandpa Odd's presence. "Hush!" I hissed at him, before he could no doubt make some kind of comment. "You'd better be good."

"So you think it's good?" Rachel smiled brightly. "You really like the drink then?"

"Sure do." I nodded, thankful for the opportunity to cover. "In fact, I'll buy another one for the road, if you don't mind. And throw in a sandwich, too, with lots of turkey, and roast beef, and cheese. Seriously, no organic stuff."

"Sure, I'll get it right away." Rachel grinned.

A few moments later, I was once again headed on my way home, a bag in one hand and another smoothie (already half gone) in the other. I liked going to Rachel's. Too bad every time I showed up it seemed that *odd* man was there.

"Can I come out of here yet?" Elysian asked, his voice muffled from the inside of the backpack, and his body squashed between the textbooks.

"No." I still burned with anger at his earlier antics.

"Please? This has to be considered pet abuse."

"No it's not. My mother's a lawyer, and you can't testify anyway. We'll be back at my house in a couple of moments, would you relax?"

"Come on."

"Look, you're irritating me. Why can't you just go back to whatever radioactive sewer pipe you crawled out of and stop bothering me?"

Elysian slithered out of the backpack and dropped to the ground. "First of all, I did not crawl out of a radioactive sewer pipe. I was sent down here from the Realm of Immortality. Second, you need me. I told you this before. How else are you going to fight the evil your world now faces?"

"What evil?!" If I didn't feel so radically annoyed, I would have thought the very idea was laughable. "There is no evil! This is a postmodern society, moron. Nothing is considered bad. I'm sure you've got it all wrong, whatever it is you're talking about."

Elysian sighed. "I can't believe you're really the one I was sent to find—"

"Who would send *you* along to find *me*?"

"I'll tell you everything, if you'll only give me the chance."

"I don't want to know!"

"Your ignorance is impossible to deal with!" Elysian roared, as he jumped up on his hind legs. His wings grew bigger and his body became longer and fuller. He transformed into his real dragon self. I briefly heard some young children nearby scream as Elysian tossed me onto his back and took off for the sky.

☼15☼
Beginnings

"Whoa!" I yelled in surprise as I dropped my sandwich bag. "No! I paid good money for that!" I complained, grabbing onto a pair of Elysian's horns just before I almost fell off Elysian's back.

"Be quiet!" Elysian's voice was deeper and scarier to me in his true form. He hauled me up further and further, until the city was a glimmering speck on the dirt below.

"Where are we going?" I asked a moment later. I was having trouble keeping my breath as we went higher.

Finally, Elysian slowed down, and I discovered my fear of extreme heights. "This is your world, right?"

"I suppose," I agreed, awed by the spectacular view, even as I was annoyed with my abductor. "Can we go back down to it?"

"No. Do you see the stars?"

Of course I saw the stars. Billions of them were swimming all around my vision; I was dazzled and dizzied by the twinkling lights as Elysian continued. I also remember vaguely hoping we were not on NASA's radar.

"I will tell you what happened now. This world's darkness has clouded my memory. This side of the River Veil—the River of Memory that guards immortality from humans—is hard on creatures like me."

"Well, that's too bad. You know a lack of oxygen is hard on

creatures like me, so can we just—"

"Hush. I'm talking now," Elysian interrupted, and even from his bigger body voice, I could tell there was an irritated quality to it.

"A long time ago, the earth was peaceful, and full of light. It was treasured among all worlds by the Prince of Stars. He protected the earth with his warriors."

"So he's an alien?" I asked, remembering my nicer dreams.

"No, it's never that simple, kid. He is much more. He is the one who brought the human race to this planet—it is a planet of his own design."

"You mean he made it?"

"I'm talking here." Elysian rolled his eyes.

"But that's impossible."

"You are so rude. Can't you just let me finish the story before you ask your questions?"

When I glared at him, he seemed to take it as though I had given my blessing.

"Anyway, some of his warriors, his Stars, turned on him."

"Wait. *Stars?* Stars are just huge burning balls of gas. They're not people."

Elysian huffed again, and I bit my mouth shut. Why did I want to learn about this anyway? I asked myself. *Don't buy into this. You'll be an outcast if you do. That's what happens to people who*

225

believe crazy things. And then they get sent off to asylums. You don't get to go off to college and become a lawyer if you go to the asylum. It's not like it's AA.

" … Peace of the world and all of humanity's soul was hollowed out, all because of his betrayal. We think he did it largely out of spite, but we are not sure. But there will be a day when he answers for it."

Huh? I hadn't been paying attention.

I resumed listening because I was being forced to. But no one could make me believe anything I didn't want to believe. I put my skeptical face on.

"The Prince of Stars, and his Stars of the First Light, the *Manorayashon*, fought the emptiness in order to save the people from complete destruction. The Prince and his forces were able to seal away the most deadly of their foes—the Seven Deadly Sinisters, the *Saadonrasha*, trapping them within the white-hot intensity of a bright star."

What language was he speaking now? "Wow. That sounds … really … made-up." I was about to add additional comments to my critique when I recalled the vision of the supernova. The faces of Orpheus and his rainbow of charges. The relentless figure hounding me in the back of my mind, pushed behind the shadows of my willful ignorance.

I switched back to the concerns at hand as Elysian glared at me. "I was there. I saw it myself," he declared.

As if his word was enough for me. "Well, you think weird and look weird and should be made-up, too, you know," I

226

countered.

Elysian sighed. "You are so narrow-minded. You don't believe in the impossible until you see it, smell it, run psychoanalytical tests on it, is that right?"

"So? I like knowing what's real and what's not."

Elysian sighed again. "Your delusions would be quite amusing if they weren't so sad," he told me, and I was offended. "Your perception is extremely limited. But back to what I was saying.

"The Seven Deadly Sinisters were the most powerful of all the dark forces' warriors; they were worse than humans who rebelled, because they were among the highest ranking Starlight Warriors, before they turned."

"This has got to be some kind of unwritten portion of *Star Wars* or something. You know, 'the dark side of the force.'" I laughed.

"You're stupid." Elysian smacked me with his tail. "Light and Darkness are not natural enemies—there is no such thing as dark in the sense there is such thing as light."

"*I'm* stupid? Of course there is such thing as darkness." Now I had proof Elysian was all wrong about everything he'd ever said.

Elysian narrowed his eyes. "What is darkness, but the absence of light? It is the void you should watch, because snuffing out the light is more dangerous than shielding it."

"What?" I scratched my head in confusion. "You mean—"

227

I stopped there. "Never mind. I'm not buying this. Let's just skip this part, Elysian. I'm getting hungry and tired, I've had a bad day, I don't understand, and I think I need some rest."

Elysian frowned at me. "You'll never learn the truth if you get caught up in your emotion-driven excuses," he warned.

"Well, can I just worry about it later?"

Elysian shook his head, irritated.

"Fine. Where do I fit into this whole mess?" I asked. "Just tell me and get it over with."

"You are a Star, fallen into humanity, an *Astroneshama*. And you have been chosen to capture the Sinisters once more."

"What?!" An incredulous look crossed my face. "That's not possible. I don't want to have anything to do with this, including capturing anything."

"You have to."

"But I don't want to. They're not really bothering me—"

Elysian grinned. "Oh, so that Gwen girl means nothing to you at all? You seemed pretty determined to save her from them."

I shut my mouth. Elysian had me there. "Well, so what if she does? That doesn't mean I want to protect the whole world. I'll just protect Gwen."

"What about your other friends? And your family? Your brother? Everyone you've ever known and liked, and loved, and cared for?"

"There aren't many people I care for—" I found myself grasping at straws now. "Elysian, you've got the wrong person. I mean, I know I'm a genius, and I'm strong, and I've got the looks to be a great superhero, but I don't really want to be one. I like being a sports star, someone who is admired by fans and girls and … more girls!"

"There is something greater than your own glory dependent on this," Elysian scolded me gently. "There is no doubting it's you. Your power the other night proved it."

"Well, what about that girl? That Starry Knight person? Who is she? She was able to fight off that smurf-woman. Why doesn't she protect humanity?"

"You are the one I was sent to. Never mind her destiny for now. You've got your own to worry about."

"But I can't do this! I'm just a normal—okay, extra-awesome—teenager in high school trying to graduate so I can go to college, major in pre-law and political history, and go to graduate school to become a government worker."

Elysian sighed. "I suppose everyone has the choice to accept or refuse the opportunities presented to them."

"Look, Elysian. I can't be the person you want me to be, even if you think it would be better. I've got to learn to make mistakes on my own."

"I should have known you would not say yes anyway. You have no love in your heart."

"What?" *What does that have to do with the price of tea in China?*

Elysian ignored me, continuing on, "And you have no real fighting skills; you are a long way from becoming an even decent warrior again. It's actually probably better you don't fully accept the supernatural abilities you have. With all the human influence you've been exposed to, you would only cause trouble with them."

"What?!" I found myself climbing further up onto Elysian's head. "I don't have supernatural abilities, for one thing—"

"That other night, you managed to scare away the one Sinister," Elysian reminded me.

"—and I am capable of love, so I don't really see the point of you bringing that up—"

"Everyone needs love; that is the best defense against—"

"—and I could so become the greatest warrior person ever if I did accept your stupid, made-up, not real, offer."

"Except you don't know what kind of powers you have, and it would take hard work for you to grow and mature into the kind of warrior you were made to be."

"What?" I looked down at him. "I didn't catch what you said."

Elysian snarled. "You should know, at this point, if you do not act on your given abilities, and continue to deny them, they will eventually go away. That is probably why they have remained dormant inside of you for so long."

THE STARLIGHT CHRONICLES

"That's fine."

"Once they are gone, there is little hope for getting them back," Elysian warned.

"I don't care. I don't want them. Sell them on eBay, if you want."

"Do you even know what you are giving up?"

"I'm perfectly aware that I am giving up the chance to ruin my high school career and my reputation by not accepting this."

Elysian shook his head. "Your decision to not act will cost you much more than fighting it."

"What do you mean?" That caught my attention.

"If you really want to give up, you will see," Elysian told me. "If you love the illusions you have surrounded yourself with, you will see them increase to their deadliest. You were assigned to capture the Seven Deadly Sinisters. When things meant to do a job don't work, things go horribly wrong for everyone, not just you."

I felt a strange sense of irritation and disgust—and a tingle of fear—at Elysian's words. I wondered if Elysian was trying to guilt-trip me into believing some fairy tale was real, that there really was some line drawn about good and evil and absolutes; that I was a cast away star living among normal humans; that I had a duty to humankind for something I didn't want to do, or worse yet, that he knew how to convince me.

Thankfully, it's too huge and inconvenient for me to believe it all. Or any of it.

"Just so you know," Elysian added, "being ignorant will only make you happy until you least expect it."

And that was the way I wanted it. I wanted nothing more than to be surrounded by my own ideas of the world and have the free will to choose which way I saw it, even if it was all folly. I pushed wildly at the madness in my mind, scuttling away at the gnawing ghost walking with unhurried chase and increasing desperation.

And that was probably why I missed the fact, as we were headed back down to Apollo City, that there was a deadly, brilliant ring of sunshine burning a hole in the clouds above my city.

☼16☼
Fire

Elysian was a persistent devil with the whole saving the world stuff. As the days passed by, I'd gotten used to his arguments more or less, and managed to keep the guilt down when he'd read the news headlines from my computer and wonder aloud if it was something to do with the Sinisters or other fallen Stars.

They became part of the routine, something my dreams and visions and soul-stirrings never quite managed to do. That was why, the following Friday, when I woke up in a cold sweat, I placed my hand over my heart as it felt as though it was trying to pop right out of my body.

That dream again. It was that supernova dream.

I blamed the spells on Elysian, who was quietly and oh-so-innocently sleeping on the edge of my bed. *But even that didn't make sense*, a small part of my brain told me. *The dreams had come long before Elysian sought me out.*

I ignored that part of my brain; Elysian was a too-convenient choice for a scapegoat.

Elysian opened his eyes. "Big day today, isn't it?" he asked. Already the sleepiness had left him, and I was slightly jealous of that. (Although I was ready to call it suspicion to make myself feel and look better.)

"Yeah, the last game of the season is today," I replied. "And then next week, swim team practice starts."

"You just go from one sport to the next?"

"Pretty much."

"Oh, I see. How sad for you."

"What do you mean?" I asked as I ruffled around trying to find my books and homework.

"You just go from one season to the next, one plan after another. You're not a very spontaneous kind of person, are you?"

"I have priorities," I told him, and myself, while reaching for my socks, "but that doesn't mean I can't have fun."

"I don't imagine you have a problem with fun," Elysian replied. "It's the lack of control I mean. You like being in control."

"Well, yeah. Of course." Duh.

"You have your whole life planned out, at age sixteen—"

"Closer to seventeen—"

"And it's just one big fat to-do list." Elysian looked up at me meaningfully. "No wonder you don't believe in the supernatural. You don't have the time to spare to consider it, you're so busy and stressed, trying to control everything."

I looked down at him. "So? It's my life."

"I know. But it just seems, well … you're afraid."

"Afraid of what?"

"Afraid of taking a risk—of believing in a higher purpose, not to mention a better one than the one you've planned out for yourself."

I was about to hotly deny I was afraid of anything when Cheryl called up, "Hamilton! I'm going to work now! Make sure you leave on time!"

I sighed. "This is not about you. My life has nothing to do with you," I told Elysian. "I don't want to hear this anymore."

"But aren't you the least bit curious?"

I stopped in my tracks. I glanced suspiciously at the small dragon, with a half-annoyed, half-intrigued look on my face. "Curious about what?"

Elysian grinned. "About your powers? About your mission?"

I huffed and turned away, about to leave once more.

"About Starry Knight?"

That one caught my attention. I swiveled around. "What about her?" I asked. "Do you know who she is?"

"Ah … " Elysian had a look on his face that made me want to punch him. "So, you are curious. You want to know who she is."

I folded my arms across my chest. "So you don't know," I countered.

Elysian frowned, staring at me for a long moment. Then he grinned and shrugged. "Nope."

I could've kicked myself for revealing my weakness. I *was* curious about Starry Knight. I could hear the taunting remarks from Elysian already. "I'm out of here."

"Just remember what I told you. Ignorance will make you happy until you least expect it."

I grabbed my backpack. "Stay here today. I'll be back home after school tonight."

Elysian cringed inwardly as the door slammed behind me. "That boy does not like being pestered to do the right thing," I heard him mutter. "What do you suppose I do now?"

Who is he talking to? I wondered. But I shrugged it off. *Great,* I thought. *I've gone crazy, and now so have my imaginary friends.*

It was hot out. Hotter than most days, especially for November. And it wouldn't help being inside, either; Apollo Central was too cheap for air conditioning.

I wiped the sweat off my forehead before I rubbed my sore back. I sighed as I tried to control my anger. Elysian was a major pest. Imagine the nerve of some lizard coming into my life and telling me there was some battle between good and evil that I had to worry about.

And who was this Starry Knight person, anyway? Today had been the first time Elysian even mentioned her. I suddenly wondered if Elysian was telling the truth when he said he didn't know who she was. And why should I trust him? I certainly had no reason for doing so.

"Hey, Dinger," Poncey greeted me gloomily.

"What's up, Poncey?" Poncey looked sick today, really sick.

"Martha's giving back the tests today. I think it's going to ruin my weekend."

"Aw, don't worry about it so much. You'll see."

"I'm not as smart as you," Poncey reminded me needlessly.

"So? You're not the only one." I smirked.

Poncey shook his head. "Never mind." Poncey pulled out his Game Pac and started playing. "There'll be no making fun of Martha today." He sighed.

Drew and Jason came in and sat down. "Hey, Dinger, guess who's in trouble with Gwen?" Drew asked. "Jason and I just heard her telling Tim to leave her alone."

"I told you Bunny-face Tim was a loser," I reminded them. "I'm glad Gwen's beginning to see the light."

"Well, they only had a fight, just so you know," Jason clarified.

"I don't really care," I replied easily enough. "Tim's not good enough for Gwen. She deserves the best out there, and

I'm sorry if I just happen to be the best. Oh, wait … I'm not sorry. She'll be done with him when pity is replaced by annoyance and irritation, I'm sure of it." A twinge of pain snaked up my back, and I had to bite back a groan. Speaking of annoyance and irritation.

Mrs. Smithe walked briskly into the room. "Good morning class," she greeted. "I know you are excited it's Friday." She looked at us intently. "Today, I will give back your exams at the end of class, so you can pay attention to the lecture and take extensive notes. I was extremely disappointed in the grades for the exam, but seeing as how it came as a result of last week's weather issues, I have decided to curve it. No one person got a hundred on it, just so you know."

Half of the class (my side) gasped. They all turned and looked at me. I grinned. "I felt sorry for all of you." I smirked. "So I missed a couple on purpose."

Mrs. Smithe shook her head. "You and your ego can't both fit into this room, Dinger," she warned.

"Come on, Mrs. Smithe, just trying to be honest." I smiled.

"I guess that's a good character trait to have," Mrs. Smithe agreed. "So I'll be honest. You were not the one to set the curve this time. Hoshi was."

The class (this time all of them) gasped.

I shrugged. "I was just trying to do all of you a favor," I muttered, with something like anger behind my words.

"Well, now that's settled, let's talk about the Civil War

238

Era!" Mrs. Smithe clapped her hands and headed for the board.

For some unknown reason, I decided to pay attention in class today—or least try.

Class passed by slowly, and it seemed like the room was stuffier than usual. As I was leaving the room, Mrs. Smithe called out to me, "Hey, Dinger, get over here for a sec."

I almost dragged myself over to her desk. "Yes, Mrs. Smithe?" I asked, trying my best to smile brightly, despite myself. I had a feeling I knew what is coming.

"I wanted to ask you if everything was going all right," she told me bluntly. "I know you put up quite a front. You seem, well, not yourself."

"I'm perfectly fine, Mrs. Smithe—"

"Don't give me that," Mrs. Smithe responded. "I'm in charge of the Mock Trial Team here. Prove it."

"But I'm fine. See? All here." I threw out my hands, almost in exasperation.

The rim of her thick glasses glimmered. She just looked at me with that intense stare for a long moment. I felt my breath catch. She wasn't buying it. Crap.

But then she sighed, surprisingly relenting. "I will not make you tell me, of course, what is bothering you. Denial never makes the problems go away; if anything, it usually makes things worse."

That's more or less what Elysian said before, I thought glumly. I respected Mrs. Smithe, probably more than most people, and here she was telling me the things I wanted to hear the least.

Mrs. Smithe scooted her chair back and sighed again. "Well, hopefully, you'll be a bit brighter later tonight. I was thinking of coming to the game."

"Uh-huh."

"I see you're not impressed. Well, in any case, if you need anything or just want to talk, or think, I can help with something, come and see me."

"Thanks, Mrs. Smithe." I smiled—genuinely—up at her.

"By the way, Dinger, what did you think of your test grade?" she asked as I headed out the door.

"Everyone's got to get a ninety-seven percent in their lives sometimes, I suppose."

She grinned. "Go and get to class, Dinger. You're going to be late."

"Hammy!"

I turned around to see Gwen. "Hey," My mood suddenly picked up despite the oppressive nature of the atmosphere today.

"Hi." Gwen blushed as she came up next to me. "I was hoping to catch you before the game today."

I smiled. "Are you coming? It's the last one of the season."

"No playoffs?" Gwen asked.

"No," I remarked bitterly. "We didn't get in. A couple games being canceled damaged our record pretty bad." I didn't want to mention Homecoming had a lot to do with it, too. (It was still too painful.)

"I see." Gwen's voice was softer now. "I'm sorry."

"It's all right. College scouts don't usually pay attention to sophomores anyway," I told her. "I'll be fine."

"You want to go to college to play football?"

"No, but it'll help me get a scholarship to a good university," I remarked.

"Oh, I see." Gwen nodded. "Do you mind if I walk home with you?"

"No, not at all." I grinned. She turned away and looked down. "What's wrong?"

"Nothing is wrong," Gwen assured me.

Recalling how I'd answered the same question from Mrs. Smithe, I raised an eyebrow at her, skeptically. "Oh, come on. You can't expect me to believe that."

"Well … " Gwen sighed. "I should've known you would know. It's Tim."

"Is that loser annoying you?" I demanded to know. "I'll get him beat up, if he's been bugging you."

"No, it's not that," she said. "Please don't bother him. He's just … well, I don't think you should know. I like him and everything, you know. But I'm wondering … we're just … I don't know, I guess."

"But you're happy, right?"

She looked over at me and smiled. "Hammy, you're so silly." She giggled.

"What do you mean?" I asked, more than a little irritated. I hated it when people laughed at me for being nice. (It's one of the reasons it didn't happen a lot.)

She grinned. "I'm sorry for laughing," she apologized. "But you can't expect me to believe happiness is the most important thing, right?"

"It's a big part of it," I reminded her.

"I know. But it's not *the* most important part in any relationship. It might be a benefit, but love isn't always happy. If I left someone every time I was unhappy with them, well, *we* wouldn't be friends right now," she told me.

I said nothing as we continued to walk toward Gwen's house in silence. *That's what she thinks?* Boy, she was … definitely out there. That was the nicest way of putting it from my perspective.

My own personal peace and happiness, I decided, were key in my relationships. And that was more than perfectly reasonable to me. Why would I even consider dating someone if she wasn't going to make me happy every day and every hour of my life? I rolled my eyes off to the side. "So you still like Tim, then?"

"We're friends." She paused for a moment. "And you should try to be considerate of other people's feelings when you're friends."

Again, I said nothing. It was too easy to reply to that and get hit.

"Whew," Gwen muttered. "It sure is hot out this week." Probably just changing the subject to get rid of the awkward silence.

"I know," I agreed. The heat waves were coming off the road and some of the buildings, even off in the distance. "I would've thought it would be a lot cooler. Even with the lake effect, we're not supposed to be getting ninety-degree weather in November."

"I hope this doesn't ruin the game for you," Gwen remarked thoughtfully. "Our school sure is having bad luck with weather this year."

Yeah, we sure were.

I suddenly wondered if this sudden and odd change in weather had anything to do with those people Elysian had been talking about, those Seven Deadly Sinisters, or the *Saadonrasha* or whatever they were called.

243

After all, that smurf-lady was responsible for conjuring up the week-long rainstorm last week, apparently. And I did have that dream—which I guess was not really a dream—where she was sent back out to collect more souls. Who's to say she wouldn't try to suck the souls out of people by making them weak with sunstroke?

She didn't seem active enough to be very creative.

"I mean, games were canceled because of meteors, the rainstorm last week, and now this blistering heat … it doesn't make sense. It's not natural."

Maybe it's supernatural, I thought with a sly grin on my face. Then I shook my head, scolding myself. Thinking everything unusual was not merely a coincidence, but some strange mythological creature at work, was going to drive me nuts. And I already thought I was insane enough.

Gwen giggled, drawing my attention back to her. "You know," she said, "I think my arm's been doing a lot better today. After I got home from the ACHE meeting, it was perfectly fine. My dad called the hospital. He's wondering if they switched x-rays or something."

I looked closely at her arm, surprised to see a faint glow coming from it. That glow …

Ugh, I am never going to get away from this! I screamed in my head.

I've seen that faint glow before, on the wrist of the girl in my dream. I glanced at my own marked wrist, which was carefully concealed by my football wristband. There was

244

nothing there, no glow, but I wasn't convinced everything was fine.

All of a sudden I was afraid for Gwen. She had been selected by that Maia Sinister before. Maia might've come back for her revenge already. I scrutinized her closely, relieved to see Gwen still looked like herself. A bit sweatier than usual, but still chipper, and still herself.

"I hope it's better," I said neutrally. No need to get her freaking out and thinking I was as insane as I suspected. There weren't a lot of girls that went for that "insane guy" profile when looking for a date. "I can't imagine it's fun wearing that bandage in this heat."

Gwen nodded wryly. "Another reason I want to get it off."

I glanced down at my wrist again, slightly nervous. I'd told no one about the mark on my wrist; thankfully, it was small enough to hide with my armband. When asked about it, I told my friends and parents this week that I was wearing it for good luck, but that was the worst of it so far.

And since I did want a perfect game tonight, I foolishly hoped my armband *would* grant me my wish.

But now the cursed mark underneath tainted any chance I had at happiness. The black star trickled with heat as I walked with Gwen, as if my suspicions were being confirmed.

☼17☼
Complications

"Are you home, Ham?" Mark called out, tearing at the fabric of my concentration.

"Yeah, it's me," I called out from my room. "What do you need?"

"I have bad news," Mark said as he walked to the door of my room. "Mrs. Weatherby was just admitted to the hospital. She's got that new sickness, supposedly … and it doesn't look good."

"Who … Oh, Mrs. Weatherby? Should I care?"

"She's only been Adam's nanny since he was two." Mark's eyebrow cocked up as he folded his arms and looked disappointedly at me.

Mark had this idea that just because I didn't care much about my brother's life or the other people in it, I didn't have the proper "familial spirit."

"Oh, I thought she was Adam's daycare teacher." I flopped down on my armchair. "Why's that a problem?"

"Well, I just got beeped. Mrs. Ellsworth had a relapse and needs critical emergency surgery on her heart, and I've been stuck with Adam since I got home this morning. I need you to watch him until your mother gets home."

"Aw, come on! I don't want to watch Adam." I complained. "He's barely three years old; he's not that

246

exciting."

My father frowned. "Look, Hamilton. I'm very tired, and you're probably right, Adam's not exciting for you. But he is your brother, and I need to go to work. I'll make it up to you later, all right?" With that, Mark grabbed his keys and headed for the door.

"Thanks a bunch, Mark!" I complained again, before letting out a stream of curses and death wishes.

A loud roaring noise followed by a child's shriek grabbed my attention seconds later. I groaned. "Elysian!" I yelled. "What did you do to my brother?!"

The tiny dragon huffed, smoke streaming out of his nostrils in annoyance, as he poked his head out between the stair railings. A long white bandage was wrapped around his lower body, and a couple of Band-Aids were stuck to his forehead and horns. "That kid is not afraid of me!"

"So? You want a medal or something?"

Elysian shook his head. "No, I want him to stop trying to play doctor with me!"

I looked up to see Adam, not crying or screaming, but wearing his play-doctor costume with a stethoscope hanging around his neck.

I couldn't help it. I laughed. So I finally had an idea of what to do with Elysian if he got on my nerves too much. "You mean you can't put up with playing doctor? Why don't you just pretend you're a stuffed animal or something? He'd never

247

THE STARLIGHT CHRONICLES

know the difference. Grow up."

"You're one to talk." Elysian frowned. "Who was it again, cursing and grumbling about having to babysit?"

I ignored that comment. "Can't you do something about him?"

"What do you mean? You're the one in charge of this kid," he replied.

"Well, you are some kind of magical creature, from what you've been telling me. Can't you just put him under a spell or something?"

Elysian narrowed his eyes threateningly at me as he kicked off the last of the play bandages. "You're mocking me, and I don't appreciate it, especially since you're the one who's been neglecting your duty to protect the world."

"Can't you put him to sleep?" I asked/whined. "I don't think it would hurt. Heck, with his crying, I think it would *help* the world."

"No! There are little things called "rules," you know," Elysian said. "I can't break them because you don't want to be responsible."

"There are rules? That stinks," I muttered. "What is the point of having power if you have to follow rules?"

"Are you even listening to me?" Elysian asked.

"Not really."

"I figured as much."

A few hours later, it was getting close to kick-off time. With little less than an hour to get to the school, I was starting to go crazy. Not spooky-dooky crazy, just caged-lion crazy. "What in the world is Cheryl doing?" I muttered as I once again dialed her cell phone number. When it went straight to voicemail, I nearly chucked my phone at the wall.

"What's wrong?" Elysian asked. "You should be happy. After all, your brother's been asleep for nearly an hour."

"Just how dense are you?" I asked. "There's a game in ... " My gaze went to the nearby clock hanging on the wall. "Forty-five minutes!"

Elysian waved it off. "It's too hot out to play, anyway."

"Football players are tougher than that!"

"Sheesh, calm down, would you?" Elysian muttered. "What's the problem?"

I glared at him murderously. "I can't leave Adam here with no one in the house—no human, anyway," I added as an afterthought. "Cheryl's apparently dilly-dallying around with Mr. Boss or Mrs. Booze at the moment, and can't seem to remember this game is imperative!"

"For you, maybe." Elysian sighed. "Anyway, why don't you just call Adam a babysitter?"

"I can't do that! Mark and Cheryl would kill me for throwing him with just any babysitter."

"Can you take him with you?"

"And what? Let him roam the stadium by himself? I can't do that—what if I have to go get him in the middle of the game? I'll be benched for sure."

"You really are the most self-obsessed person I've ever met," Elysian grumbled.

"I am not," I retorted. "I'm thinking of everyone else. Everyone's counting on me. Imagine how all my fans would feel if I didn't come!"

Elysian rolled his eyes. "There's always next year," he grumbled. "Besides, it might not be a bad thing you're stuck here. Remember the last time you were at a football game? If you had any common sense, you might be worried about what could happen tonight."

I stilled for a moment, remembering the people who had been just blankly staring off into space. I thought about the half-daydream I had while I was working on my homework in my room; Maia had been plotting something. But she didn't seem too eager to work.

"I don't think it will happen tonight," I said. "I didn't have a premonition about it taking place at the arena like last time."

"You mean you can see them coming? You have been given visions?"

"Sometimes, I guess." I glared at him.

"Kid, that's extraordinary. You haven't accepted any duties

250

or conditions to your intended role, but the Prince is giving you power and letting you see glimpses of other portions of time. This means," Elysian said with wide eyes, "you have maintained the promise of free will."

I snorted. "That's absurd. He'd have to be outside space and time to be able to control everything that happened to me."

When Elysian just looked at me with an irritated expression, I rolled my eyes. *Of course* this Prince guy was all-powerful. Elysian needed something big to tie his little stories all together.

"But you don't always see them coming, even with the visions, right? So it could still happen."

"Well, that's great to know. Anything could be a trap, in that case. Sounds like you're just paranoid," I remarked as I massaged my back. I didn't want to talk about it.

Elysian tilted his head to the side. "How long has your back been hurting?"

"Since last Thursday, probably because I was hurled into a school window. And into a tree," I reminded him. Elysian was studying my face and starting to smile. "So before you go and get any ideas about it, you can forget them. I'm a normal, sixteen-year-old student at Central High. Nothing more—unless you count my awesome skills and athletic ability—and nothing less."

"We'll see ... we'll see," Elysian muttered. "You know, there's a way you can tell if there was something going on. If you look at the mark under your wrist, you should be able to tell."

"What do you mean?" Remembering the incident with Gwen's arm, I froze. *The glow.* I frantically looked down at my wrist. I was just about to pull off my armband when my cell phone rang, making me jump. "Hello, Cheryl?" I asked. (For once, I desperately wanted my mother to be the one calling me.)

"No, it's Gwen." The voice on the other side of the phone line sounded amused. "I was calling to tell you my arm is better—"

"Gwen!" I interrupted her as a brilliant idea skid like lightning across my brain. "Gwen, you babysit kids, right?"

"Uh, yeah. Why?"

"Can you meet with me in twenty-five minutes?"

"Yes. Why? What do you want?"

"I need you to do a huge favor for me." I grinned, glancing up the stairs with a bright gleam in my eye. "Call it your way of thanking me for saving your life."

☼18☼
Assaulted

I seriously doubted I had ever run faster in my life as I headed toward the school. With my little brother clinging to my shoulders, I sped up as I caught sight of Gwen. We'd agreed to meet in Shoreside Park, where she would take Adam off my hands for the duration of the game, and I'd get to walk to the game with her. (It's an unofficial way for football players to announce they had a date.)

"Gwen!" Her auburn hair was shining in the over-heated sun as I waved. I faltered for a moment, struck by the pretty picture she made. Her hair, every strand perfectly arranged, was a wondrous shade of autumn, even as her honey-brown eyes carried all the warmth of summer. Even now, she looked perfect, like nature had planted her among the beauty of the park just to add to the world's cheerfulness.

Then I noticed someone was with her. And that someone was none other than Tim Ryder.

Well, this should be interesting, I thought.

I knew I didn't have long, so I had to hurry Tim along. I jogged over even more quickly, and a moment later I was close enough to where I could hear their conversation.

"You've been avoiding me all week," Tim was saying.

I slowed as I groaned. What a baby. Can't be away from his stairway to popularity a week without feeling neglected. Doesn't he know fame is fickle?

"I don't know what you're talking about," Gwen told him.

Tim touched her arm. "Are you mad at me?" he asked. "Did I do something to make you upset? If you tell me, I'll be able to straighten it out."

Ha! He couldn't straighten out a ruler, I thought.

"I just ... well, I've been a little confused lately. And I don't think my dad likes you, to be perfectly honest." (That was a gracious understatement. After Gwen and her parents had all arrived at home from the hospital, her dad had complained that his daughter liked a wimpy ballet boy, while she had the high school football champ saving her life, and they liked me much better as a potential boyfriend. Gwen told this to Laura, who blabbed about it to Samantha who told some other girls, who told Mikey, who told me.)

Tim smiled weakly, still looking down. "Oh, I see," he remarked. "You like Dinger."

Heck yeah she does. Loser.

"I used to like him a lot," Gwen (finally!) admitted. "I had a crush on him when I was on the cheerleading squad. Don't look at me like that, Tim! It's practically a rite of passage for a cheerleader! And he did save my life. Twice."

I stopped briefly to catch my breath—I didn't want to look weak in front of Gwen or Tim now. I could've really used a hero's entrance. And I more than wanted to hear the rest of the conversation.

"I know you're a good person," Gwen continued. "I'm just

a little … " Her voice trailed off as she noticed me. "Hammy."

Tim was shocked to see me there, too. "Hi there, Dinger." He waved politely, anger subtly lacing his words.

Oh boy, this is going to be fun.

It really was the most inconvenient time for Tim to be here, I thought bitterly. Still, I put on the fake smile that was able to fool a lie detector test and waved back. "Hey guys. Am I coming in at a bad time?" I asked, somewhat hopefully.

"No." Gwen smiled, ignoring the crushed looked on Tim's face. "We were just talking. What's up?"

"I need your help, Gwen," I explained.

"What for?" Tim asked.

I felt like punching him or telling him off, or doing something to make him go away. Too bad I didn't have any *real* supernatural powers, or Tim wouldn't be feeling too well at the moment—especially if he was prone to airsickness.

Tim was lucky Adam was there, and young enough to be impressionable. "I was just about to explain," I said impatiently. Turning back to Gwen, I continued on. "Since I was so helpful to you in saving your life and everything, I was wondering if you—"

"Let me go ahead and leave you guys alone," Tim interrupted. "It's clear Dinger's trying to ask you out, and I'm sure he'd be happier if I left."

He would have to ruin it for me, wouldn't he?

"Tim, you don't have to embarrass me," Gwen told him through pursed lips.

"Yeah, why don't you just go?" I asked, looking at the time. "The game's going to start in fifteen minutes. I've still got to get there and get my jersey on. We can deal with your pathetic issues later."

"Hamilton." Gwen frowned at me, clearly irritated I didn't have the patience, desire, or time to coddle Tim's feelings. Especially since he obviously didn't seem to care about mine.

Tim hunched over and headed out.

Before he could get very far, Gwen spoke up. "Wait!"

We both looked over at her in surprise; I was disgusted-surprised, and Tim was hopeful-surprised. "What is it?" I asked, trying not to snarl.

"Didn't you come here with your brother, Hammy?"

"Yeah. That's what I was trying to ask you about, before I was so rudely—"

"Ham!" Gwen threw up her hands. "My goodness, let it go. Anyway, he's gone."

"Who?" Tim asked, turning around once more.

"Hammy's brother. He's not here anymore."

I jerked around. It became painfully clear within seconds Gwen was right. I groaned loudly. "No, this can't be

256

happening! There isn't enough time for this! I've got to get to the game!"

"You're so selfish." Tim shook his head. "Don't you think your brother is scared? I can't imagine how he feels right now, all alone and frightened."

Yeah, frightened of your ugly face, probably, I wanted to say. "We've got to find him, fast. I need someone to watch him while the game is going on so I can play."

"All right. You go look over in that direction," Gwen instructed me, pointing. She turned to Tim. "Will you help us?" she asked.

He should. It was his fault Adam was lost in the first place.

As Tim nodded, Gwen tugged on his sleeve taking him toward one end of the park, while I turned to the nearby woods.

I normally would've been sick at Gwen's egregious generosity if I hadn't been so worried about my brother, and by extension, my life. Cheryl would kill me if anything happened to him.

"Adam!" I called out. I swear, if that kid wasn't my brother, I'd probably kill him myself.

Elysian poked his head out of my backpack. "Your backpack's starting to get wet from your sweat," he complained.

"Elysian! I don't have time for your whining." I snubbed him. "Adam decided to get lost. I don't know where he went.

He could be anywhere."

Elysian jumped out of the backpack and onto the ground. "I'll go and help look for him over this way." He hurried off before I could tell him Gwen and Tim were already looking over there. *Elysian is too fast for his own good sometimes*, I thought, half in admiration, half in aggravation.

I was just about to go over and rifle through the bushes when a prickly feeling on the underside of my arm spiked my nerves. "Huh?" I looked down to see the four-point star on my wrist was *glowing*.

It was an unfortunate confirmation. "Oh, great, what's going to happen now?"

A moment later, I heard a familiar scream pierce the evening skies. There was no time to think. "Gwen!" I yelled.

A rustling sound behind me caused me to look up; Elysian poked his head out of the bushes. "Your friend is in trouble," he announced.

"Is she okay?" I asked, a little hesitant to know the truth.

"She won't be if you just stand there!" Elysian huffed at me. The small dragon started to transform into his larger self. "Come, we must go!" His wings popped out of the scaly sea on his back, and he took off.

I nodded and started to run, following the shadow of the flying dragon.

It was not long before I saw Gwen's bright tresses through the trees.

"No, please, no!" Gwen was screaming. Another one of Maia's hideous monsters, no doubt.

I could see Gwen blink the sweat out of her eyes as she dodged another attack. She tripped and fell, rolling over the ground.

"Gwen!" Tim shouted. "Let's run for it!" Pulling on her, he practically dragged her across the grass.

I watched as my run slowed to canter, and then to a walk, and then to nothing at all. Maia suddenly appeared, blocking their path. "Augh!" Tim yelled. "This way!" He redirected his steps, heading back the other way.

I almost had to laugh; if the danger wasn't real, it would've been hilarious to watch him tug Gwen around the park. He wasn't doing himself any favor, treating her so roughly.

"Oh, pardon me." Maia grinned as she called forth her power. A nice-sized sizzling ball of energy began forming in her hand. "I hate to be in your way."

Tim and Gwen stopped in their tracks. They knew they were in serious danger; they had the one ugly thing coming from one direction, and the blue lady staring ominously at them from the other.

"Do you remember me?" Maia called out with a smile.

"Do you know this lady?" I could barely hear Tim ask.

"She's the one who attacked all those people at the play!"

Maia laughed. "Of course it was me; all those people were

259

very helpful—but I never did get a chance to collect your contribution to my grand purpose."

"Leave her alone!" Tim scowled, taking out his cell phone. "Or I'll call the police."

Maia laughed harder. "You stupid boy! There is nothing you humans can do to stop me!" With that, Maia released her attack on the two of them.

Tim pushed Gwen back just as it hit.

"Tim!" Gwen screamed as he convulsed, the power tearing at the flesh of his chest. "No!"

I couldn't see him from my angle, but I could just make out a rasping, "Gwen … " before he slumped over.

"Tim!" Gwen hugged him to herself as she started to cry.

And while this was happening, I stood there, paralyzed to the point it hurt to breathe. I watched through the trees as Maia's power continued to gravitate around Tim.

I couldn't feel my legs, I noticed. And had I just peed myself, or were my legs just uber sweaty all of a sudden?

Apparently, I'd arrived just in time to overdose on fear.

"Hamilton!" Elysian huffed. "Aren't you going to do anything?"

"Uh … " I couldn't even seem to speak. It was like my tongue was swollen or my voice had been swallowed. My body started to shake as Maia continued to taunt Tim and

Gwen with her power, this time hitting Gwen as well.

Gwen screamed again, this time with pain more than surprise.

I was stuck; salty water had gotten in my eyes somehow, and I still couldn't seem to move. *Someone had to do something*, I thought, but there was no way I could.

I didn't know the first thing about my so-called supernatural abilities. What would happen if my powers weren't enough? And how would I stop them anyway? Would I have to kill them? I didn't really want to kill anything, even if they were killers themselves. What could I do?

"Hamilton!"

"I … can't! I can't do this, Elysian!" I finally blurted out. Ashamed of myself, I turned my back on my friends and started to run away.

Elysian sighed. He looked up heavenward and asked, "Is this some kind of test?!" before he slithered out of the bushes in the opposite direction I was headed. "Fine! Even if my sad excuse of a charge won't fight, I will!"

I ran until I couldn't see. Tears were welling up in my eyes uncontrollably. I finally stopped running altogether as they poured down my face.

I slumped over in the grass, trying to block out the sound of Gwen's screaming and Tim's whimpering. *This was not what I wanted*, I thought desperately. It had to be another bad dream or a hallucination. *This can't be real!* I screamed in my head, still unsuccessfully able to hear.

I felt the fear shake through my body, painfully, guiltily, stirring me up all the way from my head to my fingertips.

I didn't want to fight, as much as I knew I should. I didn't want this to be real, as much as I knew it was. The ominous shadow of light was hovering closer.

There was nothing I could do. I was done for. I would just die.

I cuddled up on the grass and hit the ground with my fists, angry at things for not being as I wanted them to be, or at least how I'd thought they were supposed to be. "This isn't fair!" I cried.

The truth is not always easy to take.

"Kid!" Elysian was calling out for me. "Where are you?"

Trapped in the dark corners of my mind, I barely heard Elysian calling, but there was nothing I could do or say. *It's happening*, I thought.

THE STARLIGHT CHRONICLES

My powers, even though I'd never known them or even really wanted them, were surely leaving, taking hope of ever knowing the truth. My own truth was about to become a lie that would be the truth to me forever—my last defense against the relentless pursuer, the ghost who haunts me even as I try to run from him …

I don't want this, I thought again, as I sunk further into despair. *I don't want this at all.*

And yet …

There was a part of me that wished I could. I wished I could've wanted this. But I couldn't. *I didn't know.* I didn't know what to do. There was nothing that I could do. I couldn't do this.

It's all right, something inside of me whispered. I felt the lies tangling around me, settling into my skin like new clothes. I felt my consciousness further slipping away from me, as though I were suddenly watching myself sleep. The voices, at the heart of the emptiness inside continued to whisper—comforting me, soothing me, telling me my happiness *was* the most important thing, the *only* thing …

"Kid!" Elysian called out again; this time it was louder.

Don't listen to that ugly dragon, the voices insisted. *He is full of nonsense, stories and fairy tales …*

I heard Gwen scream for help again, but my relentless hesitancy refused to let me move. Time seemed to stand still, as though I was frozen. I couldn't help it; nothing was more important to me than myself.

"Hamilton! Your friends need you!"

I cringed, torn between retreating further and going back.

Couldn't they understand? I didn't know who to listen to anymore! All my life, the world had said everything was relative, there were no absolutes, certainly no good or evil, there were no miracles, fate was a delusion, humans were here by accident, science was the way to see what was really true, I was in control ... all these things, I'd believed, and heard, and experienced for myself ... but now ... now it was all circumstantial.

Either choice I went with would call for sacrifice on my part.

I started to breathe more heavily. "I ... can't do this ... "

Calm down, the voice inside said. *It'll be all over in a moment, just allow yourself to relax ...*

But I don't listen this time.

"I ... am afraid," I admitted. Somehow, the hold on me seemed to grow weaker. "I am afraid to fight."

"Kid! Are you listening to me?!" Elysian called out.

I opened my eyes, slowly. The grass gradually came into focus. "I need help." Realization dawned. "I need help to fight. I need help to save my friends. I can't do this on my own!"

All of a sudden, the wind blew back, shaking through the trees, stripping my world of all traces of blurriness and bleariness. The leaves scattered all around, and I was caught up in a burst of light.

My mouth gaped open. "Huh?" I stood up, wiping my hands on my jeans and looking around. The woods had just been filled with a blinding, warm light.

Then I understood.

My fear had been covered up by the world's lies, but the truth was breaking through, like the breaking dawn after twilight.

I gasped as the light, blazing, pierced straight through to my heart.

And then I saw him. The one who had been pursuing me.

A man with bronze skin and fiery eyes, who wore a golden crown on his white hair … The man wasn't old, but he was not young; he seemed beyond time, beyond measure, somehow. I couldn't look at him directly, but the picture was burned into my mind with startling clarity.

The man smiled gently, like a friend from long ago. "Rise up, and believe," he whispered. "I am here with you." He pointed to my right hand; I looked down to see my mark glowing again. I glanced back up, wanting to ask him the questions for which I had no words.

The one that did manage to leak out was, "Who are you?"

It sounded so hollow and weak *I* would've hit myself. But the man just looked at me and said, "Who do you say I am?"

He was the Prince, of course. Elysian's fairy tale prince; the ruler of Stars, protector and keeper of Earth.

But who was he to me? I could recognize the face, but I couldn't name the reason I knew him, or understand why he would come and see me.

Then the strange vision melted away, and the lies I had been afraid to face peeled off like dead skin. All the greatness I'd ascribed to myself over the year slithered off me, and for the briefest second, I got a good look at myself.

It was not pretty at first. Selfishness, pettiness, materialism, whininess, anger, frustration, stubbornness, hatefulness …like rejected crayon colors, they all flew away from my coloring, melting into rejuvenating hues.

The thoughts of a different time and place stirred in my mind—not dreams, but memories. All the powers of the world and creation swam before my eyes, all wrapped up in a grand river of beauty. Light and music danced inside, resounding through my soul as incredible things—things no one had ever before seen or heard—tore through my heart, displaying the breadth and width and depth of my home, in the Celestial Kingdom of the Immortal Realm. Memories of another life—no, of another *part* of my life—as an *Astroneshama* …

The reality of everything cloaked me with a renewed sort of skin as my heart burst with a stream of power, full of truth and light. The worlds before my eyes winked away, pulling all of the wondrous imagery through like the rushing wildness of a shooting star, dropping me off in my human body, in my human feet, back on Earth, leaving me feeling both more human and less human than I'd ever felt. My back tingled painfully—but not entirely unpleasant—as a pair of wings finally sprouted. And then I found myself wearing thin but durable black armor and a red tunic, with black half-gloves on my hands. Strange, but not foreign to me.

There was no going back. I had accepted my battle, along with the consequences of embracing the truth. I suddenly wondered why I'd been so afraid of the truth.

"Hamilton!"

I smiled and turned around. "I'm here, Elysian!" I called back. "And I'm ready to fight!"

Elysian stopped in his tracks. "It's you!" he cried with joy. Then a second later, after his awe apparently wore off, he started to snicker. "I was starting to worry, kid." Then his snickering broke into full-fledged laughter.

"What?" I asked, irritated.

"I like the wingdings." The dragon laughed heartily. "They add a nice touch."

"Huh?" I reached up and felt the small pair of feathery wings arranged into a crown-like shape on my head. I sighed, glaring down at Elysian. "At least I'm not as ugly as you," I huffed.

☼19☼
Fight Back

I was surprised to find Maia and Starry Knight fighting hard against each other when I arrived back on the scene.

When did Starry Knight get here? I wondered as I stopped for a moment to watch the pretty fighter let out another one of her arrows. I shook my head almost immediately. *What am I thinking?* She wasn't that pretty. And she wasn't very nice. In fact, I really didn't know anything about her … My thoughts went down this trail for a while until Elysian slithered over to me.

There must be some adversity in my look because Elysian snarled at me. "What?" he asked. "Be glad she's here. If she hadn't come, I wouldn't have been able to go get you and protect your friends from Shezape."

"Huh? Shezape?"

Elysian rolled his eyes exasperatedly. "The *eela*!" When he saw this meant nothing to me, really, he added, "The monster over there."

"Oh." That clarified a lot.

"So, you want to get going, there?"

"Just trying to think of a plan."

"I suggest you think faster!" Elysian exclaimed, jumping out of the way of a random attack. He took to the skies to help Starry Knight defeat the Deadly Sinister.

I looked around uneasily. *What should I do?* Seeing Tim lying on the ground, unconscious, and Gwen at the mercy of the other demonic creature, I quickly decided protecting Gwen was a good place to start.

All right. Let's see what I can really do with this superpower stuff.

I stepped forward. *Deep breath.* "Let the girl go!"

Shezape glared at me before laughing. "Who are you supposed to be?" he asked. "Halloween's been over on this pathetic planet for weeks now. You don't scare me."

"Well, we'll just have to fix that!" I yelled as I charged forward. *Like a running tackle*, I thought, as I aimed for the legs.

Shezape tumbled over, loosening his grip on Gwen, allowing me to tackle him.

"Augh!" the demon cried. A surge of power burst out from him as he tried to force me off his back. There were sparks of yellow and gold flying out from him as he tried to get up. I gritted my teeth and tried to meet him, power for power.

Come on, I thought desperately. *Do the light flashy-thing!*

A stream of bright lights blasted out of my hands a moment later, and I rejoiced.

While I unleashed my untrained fury on Shezape, I saw Gwen crawling her way over to Tim's side. She cuddled him up to her chest, trying to protect him as the two fights on either side of her continued.

She was certainly admirable, even if it was a tad revolting to me that Tim was the one on the receiving end of her graciousness.

I caught her eyes with mine, and I saw a flicker of shock, and maybe even a spark of attraction. (I was hoping.)

"Wow." Gwen smiled. "There are two of them! How awesome is that?"

"Augh!" I cried out as Shezape strangled me in a sudden deadlock position. Gripping onto the monster's large hands, I fought off all the pain Shezape was causing me with his own will.

The monster slowly managed a grin. "You're not getting tired, are you?" he asked me.

"No." I snorted indignantly. "You're not getting smarter, are you?"

Shezape frowned and unleashed even more power. "You don't know who it is you're dealing with, silly child!" he cried out. "I am Shezape, the sun demon!"

I squeezed my eyes shut as I tentatively blocked the new surge of power. *He's pretty strong*, I admitted despairingly. *I wish I knew how to make my powers work!*

Shezape narrowed his eyes and emitted a small, forced laugh through his gilded fangs. He was struggling to maintain himself. "I'm going to steal your Soulfire," he vowed. "After you beg for death, you'll watch as those other two humans suffer!"

"No!" I yelled. I would never allow this demon to take away anyone's soul—even if it was just Tim Ryder's.

My blood pulsed. Light poured out from my heart to my hands, penetrating and neutralizing Shezape's power. Seconds later, the demon was thrown back into a tree.

I looked down at my hands in wonder. *Did I just do that?* I marveled. *That was awesome!* I smirked down at my foe. "Ha! You lose!"

"Look out!" Elysian called.

I swiveled just in time to see Starry Knight fall out of the sky. I jumped to the rescue. She slammed into me hard, knocking me back and rolling with me across the grass. Elysian unleashed a blast of fire at Maia to distract her.

Starry Knight hurriedly pushed her body off of mine. Her long hair tickled my face. I glanced up to see into the violet depths of her eyes.

She faltered. Her lips opened in what I read as shock, and a long moment passed between us in silence.

I desperately racked my mind to find any memory of her from the other life I'd had. There was nothing, but that felt like it was off.

Then the moment passed, and Starry Knight, recalling her battle, hurried to her feet. She pulled an arrow out and held her bow at the ready, looking threateningly down at Maia. "Enough," she commanded.

She is lovelier up close, I thought before stopping myself. Then

I shook my head again, finally standing all the way up. *She thought I was a child, remember? Weak. Helpless. Now look at me*, I thought proudly. I was a warrior, too, just like her—if not better.

"Watch it, kid!" Elysian warned me.

"Huh?" I turned around just in time to see Shezape getting ready to launch another attack.

Elysian's long, scaly tail whipped out and wrapped around the dark creature, squeezing him into submission. "Hit him!" Elysian called out.

"With pleasure." I smiled as I felt my heart jump with the adrenaline rush. Aiming carefully, I landed my punch square on.

Shezape's face caved in, his scream of pain and terror muffled as his power began fading, flaking him into dust. Elysian grinned as he tossed Shezape loose, the wind catching the speckled remains. A bright cloud of white fire with twinkling sparklers spilled all through the sky; the captured Soulfire were free.

"My Soulfire!" Maia cried out, hurrying over to the stream of souls.

"The next arrow is for you," Starry Knight called out, warning her.

Maia flipped around, a few of the collected Soulfire flames kindling in her hands. "You can't kill me with just that silly arrow!" Maia replied in a strong voice. "You might be able to banish the lesser demons, but you will need a lot more power to bind me!"

"Do you really want to test that?" Starry Knight asked.

I exchanged glances with Elysian. *What should I do?* I wondered. *What is going on?* I could tell that Elysian was thinking along the same lines.

I decided to step forward. "Stop, wait a moment!" I called out. Maia and Starry Knight looked over at me, and I slipped momentarily. Performance anxiety, I supposed.

Maia glanced back at Starry Knight and grinned.

"Kid ... " Elysian whispered. He saw the look on Maia's face. "Don't—"

It was too late. Maia unleashed a powerful energy bomb, sending it straight into the ground, creating an upheaval of dirt and debris. The earth was torn apart and flung into clouds, trembling and cracking with groaning sounds.

Elysian went flying back, finally stopping as a couple of bushes broke his fall.

Starry Knight jumped out of the way, landing on a nearby tree branch. I landed less than gracefully on my rear in a pile of mud. Soupy mud.

"Well, it's time for me to leave now," Maia called as she took flight. "So sad I have to go, bye-bye!"

"No! Come back here and fight!" Starry Knight called. She unleashed an arrow once more, but the night sky was too dark and murky for her to get a good lock on her target.

Then everything went silent; it was done.

"Eww." I cringed as I found myself ankle deep in a mud pool. *It figures.* I moaned silently. Out of all the places to land.

Elysian let out a groan as he tried to move. "That witch," he muttered. "How like a Sinister to take a cheap shot like that."

"Villains have no honor," I reminded him.

"Yeah, yeah. Quit quoting your video game mottos to me." Elysian sneered as he got up and shook the mud off his body.

"Ugh! Hey!" I complained as the mud splattered a fresh coat all over me. "This is a new outfit."

"Don't worry. You're not fit to wear it," a voice said from behind us.

"Huh?" I looked up to see Starry Knight staring down at me, her long gingerbread hair blowing in the wind. Her violet eyes were narrowed in vexation. I didn't say anything to her remark, though I normally would have.

A couple of police sirens could be heard in the distance.

"Who are you?" I asked after a moment of somewhat awkward silence.

She glared warily at me.

What? Why was she so irritated with me? Did she blame me for that Maia person getting away?

As if to answer my question, Starry Knight frowned. "Stay out of this war," she warned. "This is between me and them."

War? What did she mean, war?

I stood up and wiped the mud off of my suit. "Look," I said, trying to keep my voice level. I didn't want her mad, just annoyed. "I'm a warrior, too, and—"

She sneered. "You are hardly a warrior," she said. "You don't even know who you're fighting."

"Is it you?" I asked pointedly.

She turned and walked away. "Stay away from this battle," she warned me again. She faltered momentarily, before looking back over her shoulder. "You might get killed if you don't."

I didn't know it at the time, but that wouldn't be the first time Starry Knight would warn me off, irritate me, or insult me. It would be, however, the last time I would watch her leave without getting the last word in.

A chill ran down my spine as I watched Starry Knight left. "Well, she isn't going to be pleasant to deal with." I huffed as she took off into the night.

Elysian transformed back into his smaller self as he nodded. "She's definitely a mystery," he agreed. "We can't know whether or not she is a Starlight Warrior on our side or not. We will have to watch her. She could be dangerous."

I snorted. "Of course she is," I grumbled. She's a woman." Woman … that reminded me …

276

"Hey, where are you going?" Elysian asked as I started running.

"I've got to see if Gwen's all right."

Elysian sighed. "At least go back to your normal self, first," he reminded me.

"Uh, how?"

Elysian shuffled over. A moment later, he grinned. "Ah! The Emblem of the Prince!" he exclaimed joyfully.

When I just gave him a confused and irritated look, Elysian pointed to the mark on my wrist.

The mark had changed slightly. It was no longer just a four-point star, but two of them, crisscrossed over each other. One was glowing bright red, while the main one, the regular one, was glowing black. Elysian smiled. "That is a sign," he explained. "It means you have accepted the truth. You have been given power."

"Uh, so? How do I turn off the glowing and stuff?"

"Just touch it, kid." Elysian shrugged. "That should do it."

After pressing the mark, I was instantly reverted back to my regular self. "What a relief," I muttered. I had a sudden thought. "Elysian, do you think Starry Knight has a regular side, too?"

"You mean like you? It's possible," Elysian admitted. "But there is no doubt she is more familiar with the Immortal Realm."

"What?" I asked.

"There is no doubt she knows more than we do," Elysian repeated. "When she showed up to fight, she knew who Maia was, and who Shezape was, and what they were doing. Only a Starlight Warrior would know such things on her own."

I caught sight of Gwen. Before Elysian could explain further about stuff I didn't really get, I shook my head. "Never mind. I'll let you tell me later."

Elysian's head fell into his claws as I happily scampered over to my would-be girlfriend. "Augh!" he cried out softly, but still loud enough for me to hear. "Two steps forward, seven steps back! That's all it is with that kid!"

I smirked. Elysian was never going to be the boss of me.

☼20☼
Acceptance

"Gwen!"

She turned at the sound of her name. "Hammy."

I slowed in my running, realizing I needed a good story to tell Gwen. I didn't really want to say anything about anything.

Elysian hopped up onto my sleeve and changed from his tiny dragon self into a chameleon. "Kid," he whispered, "I wouldn't say anything about what happened if I were you."

"I'm not going to," I mumbled back. Did Elysian really think I was that stupid? "Now, shut up, or she'll realize you can talk."

I made my way over to Gwen's side. "Are you okay?"

"Yes, I'm fine, I guess," Gwen replied, sadly. "I don't know about Tim. He got hurt trying to save me."

I rolled my eyes as I saw the mushy, emotional expression in Gwen's eyes. It looked like I still had a bit of a bumpy road ahead of me if I was going to win over Gwen's heart.

"Did you find Adam?"

"Huh?" Gwen's question cut through my inner turmoil like a knife through peanut butter.

"I asked you if you found your brother," Gwen said again patiently. "I don't think he was around here when I was attacked, thankfully."

"Uh ... no, I didn't find him yet. Oh great! My parents are going to kill me!"

"Well, I'm glad neither of you were nearby when the fighting broke out," Gwen replied. "That weird lady from before came back and tried to hurt me. She had another one of those really ugly creatures with her. But guess what?" She gave me this big smile. "I saw her again! Starry Knight! She came back and protected me!"

I gave her back a forced smile and nodded as she gushed about her role model. I didn't really pay any attention to her—just smiled and nodded, said "uh-huh," and smiled some more—until she started talking about the *new* superhero.

"He was really strong, and he was just so amazing," Gwen said. Her eyes glittered with admiration. "I didn't get his name, but I hope to see him again!"

I grinned to myself as Gwen radiated affection for her rescuer—*moi*, of course. *Maybe I'll like this hero business after all.*

The ambulances arrived a short moment later. While Tim was loaded up into the back of one of the ambulances, a couple of medical personnel asked Gwen if they could check her to make sure she was fine. I lounged in the far background, not wanting to have people asking me too many questions about what had happened. While I didn't think anyone would believe me, I didn't want them thinking I needed a psychological exam while the medical teams were conveniently around.

"Careful," Elysian warned me as he crept up near my ear.

"You can't keep thinking like that."

"What do you mean?" I asked innocently.

Probably too innocently, because Elysian sighed. "This isn't a joke, kid," he reminded me. "The only way you'll ever grow in power is if you learn more and practice. You can't go back to your ignorant fairy-tale dream world where it's all about you. Commitment is a major issue, Hamilton."

"Yeah, yeah." I waved him off. "I'll worry about it later." I looked back to see Gwen was sitting on her bench, a blanket draped around her shoulders. I guess she was waiting for the results of some test. Then I noticed there was a slight shadow hanging over her.

It took me a moment to realize the shadow was a person. A girl. She looked familiar, but I didn't know why.

As I watched, the girl tugged her hand, and for the first time, I noticed there was a familiar-looking little boy holding onto her.

Adam.

I decided it was time to head over.

"Oh, Adam!" Gwen leaned over and picked him up. He was small enough to fit on her lap comfortably. She turned her attention back to the girl, and I was close enough to hear her remark, "Thank you so much. He's the brother of one of my friends. We've have been looking for him. In fact, that's what we were doing when—"

The girl nodded. "I'm glad you found him then. I've got to

get home now, so will you please see he gets back to his brother?"

"Sure." Gwen smiled. "See you later."

"Bye." The girl waved and disappeared down the block before I could make my entrance.

"She's so nice." Gwen smiled. She looked down at Adam, who had a mischievous, happy look on his face. "Hammy's going to be so happy you've been found!"

"I sure am," I said, startling her as I came up beside them.

"Ham! Adam's been found." Gwen was so happy to give me the good news; I was endeared by her genuine concern for my brother.

Adam only cooed in response.

Later that night, I lay on my bed, staring at the ceiling, thinking about the day's events.

It sure hadn't been the day I'd been expecting. I'd missed the football game, and I was going to hear it from Coach Shinal and my teammates the following Monday. I'd almost lost my brother, a nice way of saying I'd almost lost my life.

So much had happened I was dizzy just thinking about it all.

282

I still didn't know if it would really change me, though I cringed at the very thought.

Three Months Later

I watched as Elysian breathed evenly, curled up at the foot of my bed. I envied Elysian, that he could sleep so soundly after what had happened. The memory of that night would stay with me for a long time. I instinctively knew this. Perhaps it would even stay forever.

It had been three months since everything happened. Only three months since my world shrunk and was eaten viciously and voraciously by another. Three months since my comfort zone had suddenly burst into a war zone for some interdimensional dispute.

It had taken me three months, but I knew for certain, at last. I'd accepted the truth of something I didn't even really know how to explain.

I could see the chasm, the beginning of the bridge in my heart, by which I might get back—back to what, I could only guess. But there was no mistaking the murmur of certainty running along my thoughts as I curled up to sleep that night.

I was certain, after the battle with Daikan had at last been laid to rest, and the press had been averted, that I would likely never be able to go back to my own world, where it was free of worry, and battles, Elysian's snoring, Starry Knight's starry eyes and annoying smirk. It was a certainty born of knowledge and nurtured with acceptance, despite reluctance.

I'd learned there was a higher purpose in my life than going to college and getting a degree; that some things in life could be miraculous. (Such as how someone who wanted to save the world could be so irritating at the same time.)

That there was a world beyond me out there; one I couldn't see or touch, but one I could know by the brief inklings of my heart and the small stirrings of my soul.

That there was someone out there who had marked me as his own for purposes I couldn't fully grasp, for reasons I will likely never comprehend—but for something that *was* right, far more than feeling right.

Maybe that was the most important truth of all. Or maybe it was the beginning of a journey that would lead me to it.

It feels strange, I thought, as I turned over on my stomach, *to see things the way I see them now*. I yawned, ready to go to sleep at last. Ironically, I felt like I'd only been asleep until now; now, I knew the illusions and ideas I'd had before were not really the truth, and the truth was not always clear. But it was there, slowly being revealed, like the world after a dream.

C. S. Johnson is the author of several young adult novels, including sci-fi and fantasy adventures such as *The Starlight Chronicles* series, the *Once Upon a Princess* saga, and the *Divine Space Pirates* trilogy. With a gift for sarcasm and an apologetic heart, she currently lives in Atlanta with her family.

AUTHOR'S NOTE

Dear Reader,

In the original 2012 publication of *Slumbering*, courtesy of WestBow Press and MTL Munce Magazine, I started off by acknowledging a universal principle in life: There are many joys in life, but none is so pleasing as that of revenge. I think that still true today, as I sit here and write this, thinking about all the journeys this book's creation has led me through. But the glory of revenge is short-lived, like all joys this side of time, and the sentiment that had tainted the first publication has grown.

I still sit back and think about my experience with high school, about how good things and bad things came from it, and I am strongly reminded of Hamilton's own remark about how hating something entirely is hard when some good comes out of it. Despite the fear, I found my voice.

Time has passed, but the heart of this story remains. *Slumbering* reflects on one main issue—belief—and two critical responses: Spiritual battles and the ignorance with which the majority of us face it. Hamilton's spirit, in the sense where he would desire good for all humanity and for the greatest good found only on the other side of time, is "sleeping." He is only concerned with himself and his own personal happiness, health, and affluence. And he doesn't want to believe anything otherwise. Why do we believe what we believe? Usually, simply because we want to, and Ham is no exception to that matter. Don't get me wrong—Hamilton is my favorite character, no question. I love him because he's so … ironic. Hateable, but loveable, too. Infuriating and stubborn, cynical and egotistical, who wouldn't love him and hate him? And love to hate him?

Time has also shown that the same people who carried me through the publication process before are still the ones I need to thank the most. Chelsea, Ryan, and my mother all top the list. They've been very supportive, even with the big changes I've had in the last couple of years—I've moved, changed jobs, graduated grad school, and added some kiddos to my family. But I would like to acknowledge a small change: I wrote this *for* Sam, but now I've begun to write *with* God. As someone who knows the power of words, I've found this distinction to be imperative in my work.

I've also found the support of my readers and writing communities to be invaluable. Sometimes when I have moments (day-long moments, who knew it was possible?) of doubt, or fear, or seemingly insurmountable insecurity, I go to them. I reread my book's reviews. I ask for help. And it always comes. A humble thanks to everyone for their contribution, weak and insubstantial as my gratitude may seem in comparison.

Slumbering is meant to show the desire for truth and love will bring us to the one who can bring us power. I found him a long time ago, but his fingerprints on my life and its work remains. And it's all to him I owe everything. So this is dedicated first to him, and I will trust him to do what he thinks is good.

Until We Meet Again,

C. S. Johnson

287

P. S. Please read on for a sample of Book 2 in this series, *Calling.*

THE STARLIGHT CHRONICLES

AUTHOR'S ACKNOWLEDGEMENTS

EDITOR

Jennifer C. Sell

 Jennifer Clark Sell is a professional book editor and proofreader. She works from her home in Southern California. With her years of professional and personal experience, she offers several quality packages for authors. Find her at https://www.facebook.com/JenniferSellEditingService.

Photo Credit: Savannah Sell

AUTHOR'S ACKNOWLEDGEMENTS

COVER ILLUSTRATOR

Amalia Chitulescu

Amalia Iuliana Chitulescu is a digital artist from Campina, Romania. Raised in a small town, this self-taught artist has a technique which is delineated by the contrast between obscurity and enlightenment, using dark elements in a dreamy world. Her areas of expertise include the use of theatrical concepts to create a macabre and surrealistic world that still maintains a highly recognizable attachment to reality. Bridging a diaphanous environment with light elements, an eerie view, she creates a dream world of dark beauty, done with a blend of photography and digital painting. Find her at https://www.facebook.com/Amalia.Chitulescu.Digital.Art

Photo Credit: Amalia Chitulescu

C. S. JOHNSON

SAMPLE READING

Chapter 1 *from*

CALLING

BOOK TWO of *THE STARLIGHT CHRONICLES*

C. S. Johnson

THE STARLIGHT CHRONICLES

☼<u>1</u>☼
Awkward Games

"He's more awkward than a vegetarian in a meat factory!"

"He's more awkward than a democrat lowering taxes!"

"He's more awkward than a lactose-intolerant ice cream driver!"

"He's more awkward than a sumo wrestler trying to ice skate!"

"He's more awkward than Tim Ryder trying out for the football team!"

I put my fingers to my chin thoughtfully, striving to look pensive. As I pretended to think over my decision, my friends began arguing about whose answer was the best.

"Come on, Dinger, mine's perfect!"

"No way, Poncey! Can you just imagine how hard it would be to be allergic to what you're selling?"

"Jason, being lactose-intolerant isn't the same as being allergic. Gosh, you are just dumb sometimes … "

Finally I spoke up. (The moment of truth …) "All right, guys. Simon, sadly, has a valid point. I'm going to go with his answer."

As the rest of my friends let out the last of their chuckles and/or groans, I smirked in satisfy action. "Good one, Simon!" I reached out a fist bump, and my humble sap of a friend vied for it like Olympic gold. "It's a great description for Apollo City's new mayor."

It was more than appropriate, too. Mayor Stefano Mills had taken office only a few days before and already he'd been hailed as a "Politician's Politician" by already going back on his campaign promises and seeking a lot of bipartisan agreements—or "settlements," depending on which news network I happened to be overhearing.

I felt sorry for Mayor Mills more than anything else, to be honest. Our last mayor, under increasing pressure, had resigned and no one really wanted to take his place. The town council had instated Mills after a lengthy debate followed by a quick election.

"I knew you'd like mine, Dinger," Simon grinned knowingly.

"Yeah, you probably spent all week thinking of it," my sidekick, Evan von Ponce (more affectionately known as "Poncey" to us), spoke up, the teasing evident in his tone.

"Come on, mine was much better," my friend Drew McGill harped. "Can't you just see a sumo wrestler slapping the ice over and over … "

Aw. Jealousy can be so cute.

I sighed happily to myself. "Come on guys, let's start a new round. Simon's the judge this time."

While Simon tried to think of a topic for the next round of the Awkward Game, I surveyed the room much like I imagined the president did when he walked into the Oval Office. After all, it was all because of me more or less that people were here, at Gwen Kessler's surprise Sweet Sixteen.

True, my best friend Mikey Salyards had volunteered his house, since his grandma and mother were out of town for the weekend, and all my friends had invited pretty much anyone who was even decently popular. But *I'd* been the one who had thought of having the party in the first place.

The familiar faces of my friends and frenemies were paired around poor Mikey's house, looking like some sort of bizarre clique collection, laid out in no particular order. With the mountains of pizza boxes, the music of our favorite video games, TV shows, and movies, and the rush of getting together outside of school hours, it was like being in a second sort of home. A home I didn't have to worry about cleaning after everyone left.

Yes, I decided. It had been *much* too long since our last blowout.

There were good reasons for that, surprisingly none of which involved my parents. The sad lack of parties was mostly due to the last time I was at a party, when my life had inexplicably and irrevocably changed for the worst.

But I wasn't really going to think of *that* while I was at this party—I had much more pressing concerns, as usual. I was focusing all my brainpower, all my available skills, on winning the next round of the Awkward Game.

The Awkward Game is where a bunch of friends get together and make fun of people or ideas in a more intelligent way than just saying they're stupid, dumb, or ugly.

Here's how it works: One person is the judge, and the judge will call out a familiar topic. And you can pretty much call out whatever you want, whether it's the drama nerd you wish you'd never met last fall, the latest bill passed or passed over by Congress, or the latest celebrity who'd walked out of their house "accidentally" wearing leeches. Then everyone goes around and makes an awkward comparison. For example, if you pick your school librarian, you could say she is more awkward than a fruit bat sucking blood or a bald man trying to get a haircut. Finally, after everyone puts in their answers, the judge makes the decision on who has given the best response. After so many rounds, you tally up who has the most wins and that person is the winner.

I won the game a lot, needless to say. But I also relished being the judge.

Simon looked thoughtful for a moment. "Okay! I got one!" he cheered. "How awkward is Wingdinger?"

The rest of the guys laughed as I felt the fun flerb out of me. I faked a grin as the guys all began to snigger at the mention of Apollo City's "superhero."

Of course he'd go with Wingdinger. And of course, I have to sit here and take it. Nothing is going to save me from this unless by some miracle—

Splintering pain slipped around my right arm like a shackle.

Ah, there it is. Supernatural calling. I grimaced.

298

"Hey guys," I spoke up. "I'm gonna duck out this round. Gwen's over there and I want to give her my present." A round of "Oohs" and "Awws" and "Go HD!" and other unintelligible comments ensued.

Oh, what I would've given to be telling the truth.

I headed out of Mikey's house as quickly as I could. I didn't have a lot of time before Gwen headed home, and I hadn't actually had a chance to give her my present.

But my other problem, still winding its way up my right arm, had more serious potential consequences at the moment.

Keeping this at the forefront of my mind, I slipped around corner of the stairs and tiptoed towards the front door.

Why did I, the great Hamilton Dinger, the pride of Apollo City Central High, suddenly have to leave? What reason called me to sneak out away from the only bright spot of my life since winter vacation ended, jumble my way through the backstreets of the city, and head off in the direction of certain unpleasantness?

The same reason I didn't like to think of Wingdinger as awkward.

For one thing, he's me.

For another, I had a monster of some demonic nature to battle.

And then there was—

"Hammy?" There was a hand on my shoulder.

I turned around to see none other than Gwen Kessler staring at me, looking so pretty it just made the ugliness of my situation even more awful. "Gwen!" My voice went up at least an octave pitch, as if I'd swallowed Mickey Mouse and he suddenly wanted to pop up and say hi. I cleared my throat hastily. "Gwen. There you are. I was just ... "

Gwen's honey brown eyes warmed and I felt part of me melt. "Looking for me?" she ventured a lure, and I grabbed onto it.

"Yes! I was just looking for you," I agreed. "I have to ... " *I have to distract her.* "You look amazing tonight," I said.

She giggled. "Thanks."

I laughed easily, trying to force my body to relax. *Get a grip, Dinger!*

"I was just going out ... side. For a moment. It's warm in here. Don't you think it's warm in here?"

Gwen's eyes lost their sparkle. "Are you going home already, Hammy?"

I wish. "Oh. No, I just forgot to bring your present, and I wanted to go get it really quick," I assured her.

"But you're not going home? Where is it then?" Gwen looked charmingly confused.

I was getting there myself, frankly. "Oh, uh, it's at Rachel's Café," I lied. "I was there this afternoon, and I must've left my backpack there, and that's where I put your present earlier."

Gwen's brow wrinkled. "Are you doing okay, Ham? You've been acting weird lately."

"Weird? Huh. Doesn't sound like me."

"Really?" Gwen held up her hand and began counting off on her fingers. "First, you miss meeting me at Christmas, and call up the next day with some strange excuse of getting lost. Second, at New Year's, you and Mikey come over on your way to Jason's, and you leave me and Mikey hanging as you suddenly have to run home for your homework?" She giggled a bit. "I heard you've been sick during swim practice a lot too, to the point where even Coach Uzziah is getting on your back. And then, you're just so forgetful lately, it's almost like you've been avoiding me."

"Um … " I guess Gwen had noticed my rather poor run of excuses.

Ugh. I mentally slumped over in some kind of defeat. If it had been possible for time to stop for several moments, I would've spent all of it complaining about how irritating it was to be running constantly from battle to battle. 'Wingdinger' might have been needed on the interdimensional frontlines, but 'Hamilton' had a string of present obligations to fulfill. And I could only get so sick, forget so many things, or have my grandmother die so many times before people caught on.

Pain bit through my arm again, like a shackle shrinking around my wrist. I looked down to see the familiar mark on

301

my wrist glowing. Trouble was brewing. I had to go. A cringing shudder went through me. I had to go, and that meant I had to leave Gwen.

"I'm sorry, Gwen, I just have to go. Sorry," I stammered. "I'll be right back soon!" Dreading the thought of the accusing look on her face, I intentionally turned away from her as I scooted out the door, nearly tripped down the porch stairs, cursed Mikey's grandmother for needing so many safety railings, and ran away as fast as I could.

As I approached the end of the driveway, I looked to see Gwen being pulled back into the party by her best friend, Laura Nelson. The music blared out one last time, seeming to give me an extra push as I hurried away. The comforting lights of the fun-filled house diminished with distance, as did any control over my burning anger.

Awkward games indeed, I thought bitterly to myself.

READY FOR BOOK 2?

Thank you for reading! Please leave a review for this book and check for other books and updates!

THE STARLIGHT CHRONICLES